ALL SHE WANTS FOR CHRISTMAS

It wasn't exactly what Maddy had had in mind. Hugo Griffin — 'Griff' — had agreed to fly Maddy to her holiday destination but, halfway over Paradise Island, they'd been forced to crash-land! Maddy had wanted peace and quiet — but a deserted island was a little extreme. At least she had company for Christmas — Griff was the ultimate tall, dark, handsome stranger. Unfortunately, it was clear he was off limits as far as poor little rich girls were concerned.

LIZ FIELDING

ALL SHE WANTS
FOR CHRISTMAS

Complete and Unabridged

LINFORD
Leicester

First published in Great Britain in 1996

First Linford Edition
published 2011

British Library CIP Data

Fielding, Liz.
    All she wants for Christmas.- -
(Linford romance library)
    1. Love stories.
    2. Large type books.
    I. Title II. Series
    823.9'14–dc22

    ISBN 978–1–44480–565–9

Published by
F. A. Thorpe (Publishing)
Anstey, Leicestershire

Set by Words & Graphics Ltd.
Anstey, Leicestershire
Printed and bound in Great Britain by
T. J. International Ltd., Padstow, Cornwall

This book is printed on acid-free paper

1

'Is that Ursa Major?' Maddy quickly pointed to the familiar constellation as Rupert made a move to seize her hand. But he wasn't to be diverted by the diamond-spattered velvet darkness of the Caribbean sky.

'Who cares?' he demanded, and Maddy gave a startled cry as he grabbed her waist and pulled her roughly into his arms. 'You know what I want.' And with a crazy little laugh he began to plaster her face with kisses.

'Rupert,' she gasped, turning her head from side to side in an attempt to avoid his questing mouth, 'don't — '

But he wasn't taking no for an answer. 'You must know how I feel. You've set me on fire, Maddy!' he declared. 'I must have you . . . I will have you.' She was trapped, the hard stone balustrade protecting her from the sharp drop to the sea digging into her back, Rupert blocking the way to the house with his body. 'I will have you,' he repeated. 'No matter what it takes.'

'No!' she protested, desperately trying to push him away. They were supposed to be friends. Just friends. And because of that she had fallen for the oldest line in the book. 'Come and look at the stars . . . ' How on earth could she have been so stupid? 'You know you don't mean this, Rupert,' she declared, but he wasn't listening and Maddy suddenly had the most awful premonition that he did mean every word.

'I know you think I'm a fool, but I've never been more serious in my life . . . ' he proclaimed. 'I'll show you . . . ' He fumbled in his pocket and produced a heavy, ornate ring set with rubies and diamonds and held it under her nose. 'This was my grandmother's engagement ring. That's how serious I am.' He was triumphant. 'Nothing will keep me from you . . . '

He was still speaking but Maddy no longer heard him, only the shocking echo that boomed in her head . . . 'This was my grandmother's engagement ring' . . . 'my grandmother's ring . . . '

The stars began to spin, the terrace dissolve, but as Maddy swayed towards him Rupert misunderstood. He captured her hand and pushed the heavy ring onto her finger. 'I know I'm not much of a catch . . . not clever like you, but marry me and I'll make you Lady Hartnoll one day — '

The light spilling from the open doorway caught the stones and they flashed fire — hateful red fire. She tugged at the ring, hating the sight of it on her finger. 'You're right, Rupert.' Her voice seemed to come from far away, brittle and light as spun sugar. 'You're not in the least bit clever or you'd know better than to offer rubies to a redhead. You'll have to do better than your grandmother's precious bauble — '

'I'll get you another ring,' he said, a

little desperately. 'Anything you like . . .' But his words didn't register as she twisted the ring back and forth, desperate now to be rid of it, to get away, but her knuckle, broken once when she was a child and awkward ever since, refused to give up its treasure. 'You can have everything I've got, Maddy,' he insisted.

'And what's that?' Was that her laughing? Surely not. She hadn't laughed before . . . 'A second-hand ring and a second-hand title? It's not very original of you, Rupert; it's all been done before, you see . . . ' All she wanted was to lash out, hurt the man who had brought her nightmare to life . . . 'For heaven's sake, you don't even have any *real* money . . . ' For a moment there was silence. Blissful silence.

But Rupert's shocked voice broke the peace. 'My God, it's true! Charlie Duncan warned me that underneath you were as hard as nails, but I didn't believe him . . . '

'Well, you should have,' she declared

as with one final twist the ring suddenly came flying from her finger to clip his cheek, the heavy, clawed setting breaking the skin before hitting the stone floor of the terrace and rolling away into the darkness.

Rupert touched his face where the ring had struck him, staring in disbelief at the smear of blood on his fingers. Then with an anguished cry he dived to the ground and began a frantic searching for his family heirloom. This final touch of farce was too much for Maddy and a bubble of near-hysterical laughter caught her unawares. She clapped her hand over her mouth and spun quickly away, determined to make the safety of her bedroom before she gave vent to her feelings, whatever they might turn out to be. But as she turned she blundered into a figure standing in the purple shadow of the bougainvillea that tumbled about the French windows that opened from the drawing room.

The man caught her and held her as

she stumbled, his strong hands grasping her waist to steady her, and Maddy found herself looking up into a pair of fiery green eyes that for a moment regarded her with an unreadable expression that seemed to play havoc with her senses and eat into her very soul.

He was tall — he had to be if she was forced to look up at him — with the kind of dark, weather-beaten good looks that made women weep, and for a moment she remained transfixed, mesmerised, with Rupert, the terrace, the scented Mustique night all forgotten.

'You can put her down now, Griff, darling.' A cool, feminine voice brought her sharply back to earth and she turned, hardly believing her ears.

'Zoe, I didn't know you were coming to Mustique. When did you arrive? Have you rented somewhere? Stay with us . . . we've loads of room.'

Zoe glanced over her shoulder at Rupert who was by now frantically quartering the terrace in his search for the precious ring, but she made no comment. 'No, darling,' she said. 'I'm on my way to Palm Island and since the *Dragon* was on her way down there to pick up a charter I've hitched a lift. I know it's rather late to call, but we're leaving at first light and I wanted to speak to your father.'

Griff? Zoe had had a number of what she referred to as 'little flings' since her divorce ten years earlier. But this man was very different from her godmother's usual sleek, well-groomed, well-heeled companions. In his mid-thirties, casually dressed in a pair of lightweight trousers and an open-necked shirt, he was clearly much younger than her godmother, and Maddy, still held by those strong, vital hands, felt herself grow hot. 'You captain the *Dragon*?' she exclaimed quickly, pulling herself free. 'I saw her anchored off Barbados. She's very beautiful.'

'Of course he doesn't,' Zoe said, a little impatiently. 'The yacht has a full complement of crew.' So — he was just along for the ride. 'You can join us if you like.'

'No,' Maddy said, unnerved at the thought of being confined in a yacht, no matter how luxurious, with Zoe and her young lover. Then, aware that she had been a little abrupt, she added, 'It's very kind of you, but I can't leave Dad all by himself.'

'You're quite sure?' Zoe asked. Maddy found herself staring once more up into the green eyes of her god-mother's companion.

'Positive,' she said too quickly. 'Did you say your name was Griff?' she queried, the chill in her voice an attempt to disguise her sudden confusion — an intensity of feelings that she didn't fully comprehend but didn't like one bit.

'*I* didn't say anything.' His voice had a low and gravelly sound that seemed to unravel her nerve-ends. And the slightest stress on 'I' suggested that *she* had said something. Far too much. She felt the heat rise to her skin under his

8

discomfiting gaze.

'Just Griff?' she demanded pertly, in an attempt to put him in his place. Even as she said it she realised how ridiculous that was. This man wasn't 'just' anything and his 'place' would be wherever he chose.

'Hugo Griffin,' he replied formally, with the smallest of smiles. 'But Griff will do.' He extended his hand. Maddy did not want to take it, but he waited. She ran her tongue nervously over her lips and offered him her fingers, but he grasped her hand fully, holding it, swallowing it up in his own strong hand, holding it for far longer than politeness dictated. It was as if a current of electricity were being fed into her body, lighting her up. It was frightening, exciting, appalling because he was in some subtle way taunting her. She jerked her hand free and turned quickly to her godmother.

'Have you seen Father?'

'He's on the telephone.'

'Still? I don't know why he bothered

to come on holiday. Come and have a drink.'

'Don't you think you'd better stay out here and help your friend find his . . . er . . . bauble?' Maddy flushed scarlet as Griff, one brow raised the merest fraction, caught her eye. She glared at him, then glanced back at Rupert, who was now crawling about under the seating in the summer house.

'I'm sure he'll manage,' she said abruptly, and, brushing quickly past Griff, she went inside.

'I've been blown to bits driving in that wretched Moke, Maddy,' Zoe said. 'Will you point me in the direction of a mirror?'

Zoe was the most elegant woman that Maddy had ever met and she looked as if she had stepped straight from some exclusive hair salon, but Maddy didn't argue. 'You can use my room. Up the stairs and — '

'Show me the way, darling,' Zoe said, and the edge to her voice suggested that the desire for a mirror was simply an excuse to singe Maddy's ears over the scene she had just witnessed on the terrace.

Maddy turned to Griff and waved vaguely in the direction of the drinks cabinet. 'Please, help yourself . . . ' she said, and flushed once more as he regarded her with an expression that made her feel as if she had said something . . . suggestive.

★ ★ ★

'Darling, this is *gorgeous*,' Zoe said, sitting on the edge of a lace-hung four-poster bed. 'The whole house is a delight.'

'We were lucky to get a Christmas cancellation. Why don't you stay here and spend the holiday with us?'

'Christmas?' She pulled a face. 'I've never much cared for tinsel in the Tropics . . . Besides, Griff and I have something special planned. We weren't going to stop in Mustique at all, but I wanted to speak to your father and when his office told me he was here on holiday . . . ' She paused. 'What do you think of Griff?' she asked, so carelessly that Maddy's heart sank. She thought that Griff was likely to break her godmother's heart. She had never seen her so lit up, excited . . .

'Something special?' she repeated, with a sudden dreadful premonition. 'Zoe — '

'Don't ask. I know everyone will try to talk me out of it, so it's going to be a secret until afterwards . . . ' She briskly changed the subject. 'Besides, it's you who has some explaining to do. How on earth could you be so unfeeling to that poor boy? He's obviously head over heels in love with you.'

'Nonsense. He's a clown.' A stupid, sweet, foolish clown. She had told him that she couldn't be anything but his friend but he had refused to believe her, and tonight he had blundered unknowingly into a hurt that she had buried so deep that she thought she had forgotten it.

'Well, you certainly made him look like one tonight. Money's spoiled you, my girl.' Zoe took a brush from her bag and began to tidy her hair with little fidgety movements that betrayed her anger. 'You're a very beautiful young woman. But handsome is as handsome does. Just because you've been hurt once it doesn't excuse unkindness.'

'No . . .'

Zoe's face softened. 'Oh, my dear girl, I wish I could tell you, show you what you're missing — ' She stopped as she saw Maddy's face. 'Run along down and keep Griff company, darling. I can find my own way down.'

Keeping Griff company was the last thing she wanted to do, but there was something . . . 'I think I'd better go and make sure Rupert's found his . . . er . . .'

'Bauble?'

'Help yourself to anything you want,' Maddy muttered, and fled, determined, somehow, to make her peace with Rupert.

'What did you think of Zoe's new
. . . friend?' Michael Osborne enquired
of his daughter over breakfast the
following morning.

Hugo Griffin was the last person that
Maddy wanted to think about, but her
father was waiting. 'I hardly spoke to
him.' But she had been aware of his
eyes on her all the while her father had
been talking to him. 'He seems very
fond of Zoe,' she replied noncommit-
tally.

'Is he genuine, do you think? She was
asking me about selling stocks. A lot of
stocks. I've a very nasty feeling that he's
at the back of it.'

'Surely not!' She began furiously
buttering toast. 'I mean, surely she gave
you a reason for wanting to sell? Didn't
you ask her?'

'It's really none of my business,
Maddy. But she sidestepped all my
efforts to discover what was going on
with such determination that I'm

14

seriously concerned.' He shrugged. 'I just hate to see a friend, a woman at a vulnerable age, taken advantage of by some unscrupulous . . . ' He shrugged again. 'Well, I don't have to draw a picture.'

Maddy's appetite had suddenly deserted her as she remembered their brief conversation the night before, that feeling that Zoe was on the verge of something rash. 'Poor Zoe.'

Michael Osborne pulled a wry face. 'If Zoe was poor there wouldn't be a problem. I want you to try and find out what's going on.'

'How can I?' The last thing she wanted was to get involved in Zoe's romantic entanglement with Griff. 'And she wouldn't thank you for interfering,' she added quickly. 'Surely you can use your business contacts in Barbados to check up on him?'

'And if he finds out? Tells Zoe?' He shook his head. 'I'll make some discreet enquiries when I get back to London.'

'But that won't be until after

Christmas,' she pointed out. Her father pulled a face. 'Oh, I see. Your telephone call last night means you have to go home.'

'I'm sorry, sweetheart, but I've got to get back before the weekend.' He held up his hand to stall her protest. 'Don't you see? It gives me the perfect excuse to ask Zoe to have you to stay with her on Palm. After all, I can't leave you here alone over the holiday. Such a pity that Rupert had to rush off . . . ' He grinned wickedly as two bright spots stained her cheeks.

'For heaven's sake, Dad, I'm twenty-three years old, I have my own flat in the centre of London and I run my own business. I'm perfectly capable of looking after myself.'

'Of course you are. More than capable. But surely appearing to be a helpless little brat isn't too much to ask if it means protecting Zoe from some good-looking confidence trickster? I thought that you, more than anyone, would want to save a friend from that.'

'I've never flown in a seaplane before,' Maddy said in a brittle attempt to appear friendly. But she couldn't meet his eyes; instead she looked beyond Griff's sharply defined features to the small craft moored against the jetty as he lifted her luggage from the Moke.

Her father had spoken to Zoe and arranged a direct flight to Palm by seaplane. That at least had been something to look forward to. Until she'd seen who the pilot was. He tossed her bag into the tiny hold and indicated the passenger seat with a curt nod of his head. 'Unless you climb aboard instead of standing about chattering,' he informed her, 'you won't be flying on this one.'

Maddy felt her mouth nearly drop open. *Chattering!* She had merely tried to ease the almost palpable tension between them, but clearly he was furious that she was being foisted on Zoe.

Reluctantly she turned to face the man. His sea-green eyes were regarding her intently and she had the uncomfortable feeling that he was capable of peeling back the layers of her mind to discover what she was thinking. Could he possibly suspect the real reason for her visit?

She regarded him coolly from beneath long dark lashes. He was tall, with the brawny, well-tanned physique of a man who spent most of his time out of doors; his shorts, faded T-shirt and bare feet pushed into leather-thonged sandals were in stark contrast to the expensive if casual cut of the clothes he had worn when he'd come to the house — a stark contrast to the immaculate white uniforms worn by most charter pilots. He wouldn't last long with Dragonair unless he made more of an effort, she thought. Or had he other plans? There were plenty of rich widows and divorcees in the Caribbean. Women like Zoe . . . alone and vulnerable to the flattery of a good-looking man.

'Well?' he demanded, raising one sharply defined brow. 'If you've seen quite enough . . . ?' Maddy felt a blush steal over her cheekbones. He'd thought she was ogling him for heaven's sake! The sheer nerve. Flustered, she turned to the aircraft, which bobbed gently on its floats against the jetty, and indicated the fierce red dragon painted on its tail.

'Don't Dragonair pilots normally wear a uniform?' she demanded imperiously in an effort to cover her confusion.

'Normally,' he conceded. 'But who said this was a normal charter?'

'You're just doing this as a favour for Zoe on your day off? Won't your employer object?' she queried.

The expression in his eyes was unreadable against the dancing reflection of the sea, but the low, warning timbre of his voice sent a little shiver of goose-flesh rippling up her spine. 'Are you coming?'

Maddy gave an imperceptible shrug

19

and lifted her chin just a touch. 'I don't seem to have much choice. Zoe is expecting me.' If she had hoped to prod him a little with this, she signally failed.

'She didn't have much choice either, the way I heard it. After all, you mustn't be deprived of your holiday.'

'I thought you were in a hurry,' Maddy snapped crossly. Then, as she made a move to board the seaplane, it rose and fell slightly against the dock on the swell of the tide, and she hesitated.

'Afraid of getting your feet wet?' he asked.

She threw him her most withering glance, but he didn't wither. On the contrary he put two hands about her waist, lifted her from the jetty and swung her across the gap, holding her for just long enough over the space where the ocean sucked against the jetty to let her know that he was seriously considering whether to dump her in it. A little gasp escaped her lips at such brazen intimidation and, apparently satisfied that he had made his point, his mouth twisted momentarily into a tormenting little smile. Then he placed her very gently on the seat of the plane. 'I . . . I . . . ' But Maddy was finally lost for words. It was going to be hard work denting this man's composure.

Griff raised a dark brow with speaking insolence at her inability to say precisely what was on her mind. 'Yes?' he prompted.

Burningly conscious of the pressure of his fingers through the fine silk of her biscuit-coloured camisole, the invasion of the broad pads of his thumbs beneath the flare of her ribs, she was horrified to discover that she was blushing for the second time in less than five minutes. Her immune system was normally alert to all the danger signals, but this man had somehow slipped under her defences while she'd been reeling from her scene with Rupert and she was very much afraid that he knew it. She had to disabuse him of the fact, and quickly.

'One hand would have done,' she

said. It was meant as a rebuke but her voice was oddly breathy and it came out all wrong.

The lines that bracketed his mouth deepened and he very nearly smiled. 'Valuable cargo must be treated with care,' he replied.

'Valuable cargo?'

'Zoe told me that you are an heiress to a considerable fortune.'

Maddy felt a little chill invade her soul. 'Is that all she had to say?'

'She's been going on all week about how charming you are. It's odd, because she's usually so discerning . . . '

'Thank you,' she said, as crushingly as she knew how.

But he wasn't crushed either. 'Anytime, Miss Osborne,' he replied with grave formality. But at least he had removed his hands and she could breathe again.

'Now, would it be too much trouble for you to move over? You're sitting in my seat. Unless, of course,' he added, with a wry twist of his mouth, 'you

22

would prefer to fly yourself to Palm Island?'

'I . . . ' She snapped her mouth shut and scrambled across the tiny cockpit into the passenger seat. She had been about to tell him that she was perfectly capable of doing just that, and wipe that mocking smile right off his face, but she had no wish to encourage further conversation.

Besides, it wasn't strictly true. Maddy had recently obtained her pilot's licence but she'd never flown a seaplane, although the controls looked familiar enough. If the pilot had been anyone else she might even have dared to ask if she could take the controls for a while, but she wasn't about to ask 'Griff will do' for any favours. Which was probably just as well, because she was pretty sure that he wasn't in the mood to grant her any.

Nevertheless, she watched him with the fascination of the newly addicted, following every movement as he ran through his pre-flight checks, wound up the engine and then called the control tower on his radio for permission to take off.

The crackling voice on the radio gave him a heading and height and he threw her a glance to check that she had fastened her seat belt before casting off and closing the cockpit door. The snap of the lock made her jump. It had an almost ominous finality about it, as if the two of them were cast adrift from the rest of the world.

'Ready?' Griff asked.

'Yes,' she said quickly. 'Yes, of course.' She gave herself a firm mental shake and looked out of the window, determined not to say another word until they reached Palm.

Griff taxied out into the deserted bay, waiting a moment for clearance. Then he opened the throttle and, unable to help herself, she turned to watch, holding her breath as the plane surged forward under his steady hand and skimmed over the clear turquoise water for dizzy, breathless moments. Muscles flexed on strong, tanned forearms as he pulled back on the control column, their strength defined by the fine line of hairs, once presumably as dark as the untamed mop that decorated his well-shaped head but now turned to dark gold from constant exposure to the sun.

For a moment her back was pressed hard against the seat and then quite suddenly they were airborne, free, and Maddy gave a little sigh of pure pleasure that drew a brief, enquiring glance from the pilot, but she didn't notice. Maddy was staring down at the ocean, at the unfamiliar view of a string of islands that disappeared into the hazy distance, each with its own protective circle of reef.

The plane banked steeply, giving a breathtaking view of the exquisite colours of the bay beneath them, every shade of turquoise, then jade and bright emerald-green until beyond the white ruffle that betrayed the hidden reef the water turned to deepest sapphire. As they gained height a yacht, brilliant white against the sparkling blue depths of the ocean, shrank to the size of a child's plaything and Maddy had a brief glimpse of the wreck of the *Antilles* which years before had run onto the reef between Mustique and a nearby island and broken its back. Then there was nothing but a cloudless blue sky.

Maddy watched intently as Griff made the small adjustments for straight and level flight, envying the sure, confident touch of his long, sun-darkened fingers on the controls, recognising a man in his element. As if sensing that he was being watched, he turned, and for a moment their eyes, the tawny and the green, clashed

'Don't do that,' he said abruptly.

'Do what?' And she knew instantly that even thinking the question had been a mistake. Asking it out loud had been madness.

'Flirt when you don't mean it. Flash out signals like a firefly on heat. I realise there is a type of woman who can't resist the challenge but — '

'I beg your pardon?' Maddy gasped.

'I said — '

'No,' she said quickly, with a tiny gesture of dismissal. 'Forget that. I heard what you said; there's no need to repeat it.' And she snapped her head round to stare straight ahead at the achingly blue sky, painfully aware that once more she had flushed hatefully beneath her delicate tan, but this time she refused to let it go. 'You're quite wrong, you know. I wasn't trying to flirt with you.' Damn. Why on earth had she said that? Far better to have ignored it. Palm wasn't far. Much better to keep her silence. 'I was just interested in the controls.' No! No! She hadn't meant to say that! It was as if her tongue had a life of its own.

'The controls?' Griff gave a short laugh. 'Of course you were, Miss Osborne.' Before she knew what was happening he had grasped her dismissive hand and laid it over his on the control column, holding it captive, small and white between his own strong, workmanlike ones. 'Like this?' he asked, his decisive mouth far too close for comfort.

'No!' Maddy was desperate to pull free from the exhilarating touch of his hands but her brain was ignoring the urgent signals for help.

'Will you show me how you do that?' he mocked, his voice slipping easily into a fluttering, breathy impersonation of her own, so good that if she hadn't been thrown totally off balance by the swiftness of his attack, by the unexpected surge of warmth as the palm of her hand was pressed against his dark knuckles, she might just have found it funny. 'Oh, Griff, aren't you strong . . . ' His voice wavered in a perfect imitation of the kind of woman she had heard a dozen times during the past couple of weeks, the kind of woman who hung around the muscular young men who worked around the hotel and on the beaches. The kind of woman he preyed upon? If so, why wasn't he encouraging her instead of mocking her? Could it really be true that he was ready to fleece Zoe? If that was the case Griff wouldn't want Maddy telling her godmother that he had made a pass at her, would he?

He made no move to hold her as she snatched her hand away, seething with indignation. 'Maybe half the women in Mustique have thrown themselves at you, Mr 'Griff will do', she told him with considerable force, 'but, I can assure you, you are perfectly safe from me.'

'I'd be perfectly safe from you if you stripped naked and danced the limbo. I don't like heartless girls who tease.' His green eyes, hard as the heart of an emerald, flickered carelessly over her, apparently unmoved by her outburst. 'And, judging by the performance I witnessed yesterday, you're obviously a past master. Or should I say mistress?'

'Mistress?' Maddy, who prided herself on her ability to take most things in her stride, felt a flutter of confusion ripple the smooth surface of her life. Disturbed, unsettled by the man's insolent manner, she lashed back, 'Hardly that. It was doubtless his desperation to get into my bed that drove Rupert into offering marriage,' she responded vigorously, without pausing to consider the wisdom of such a statement.

'There's no need to explain; the picture came over loud and clear.' His voice was barbed. 'If you can drive a man that far you must have a rare gift for the game.'

'It's not a game,' she said stiffly, fervently wishing that she had kept to her plan to ignore him. But it was impossible to ignore him in the tiny confines of the aircraft. He reached across the small space between them to graze her mouth with the edge of his thumb and she gave a shuddering little gasp.

'Your lips drip ice, Miss Madeleine Osborne, but your eyes are on fire. A dangerous combination.' He tucked his thumb beneath her chin and forced it up so that she was looking straight up into those insolent green eyes. 'One day you'll meet someone who won't take no for an answer.'

'You?' She had intended cold mockery, derision. The word came out as a breathy little gasp, an invitation.

'Would you like to find out?' He didn't wait for her answer but reached for the dark glasses perched on the ledge above the instrument panel and slipped them on.

And, following his example, she slipped on her own sunglasses and pushed them firmly up her arrow-straight nose, signalling that as far as she was concerned the conversation was at an end. It should never have started. She wasn't so easy to provoke under the normal course of events, but this man had rattled her from the first moment she'd set eyes on him. Tease indeed! As if Rupert Hartnoll's proposal had been welcome . . . On the contrary she had been less than happy when he had arrived unexpectedly in Mustique a few days after them, especially since he had so easily persuaded her father to let him stay at the villa they had rented. But then Michael Osborne was impatient to

31

become a grandfather and, presented with a perfectly eligible suitor, he had been a more than willing accomplice.

Maddy glanced at Griff from behind the relative safety of the darkened lenses. She wasn't in the least surprised that he appealed to women like Zoe with too much money and nothing to keep them occupied. He had the kind of body any woman would find irresistible and, if not precisely handsome, his strongly moulded face and the well-defined curve of his mouth suggested a sensuality . . .

Confused at the turn her thoughts were taking, Maddy tightened her lips. Handsome is as handsome does, she reminded herself very firmly, then threw an exasperated glance at the cockpit ceiling. Oh, Zoe, she thought, why couldn't you take up knitting and grow old gracefully?

Griff reached up for the radio, speaking to traffic control to inform them that he was approaching Paradise Island.

'See you in a couple of weeks, Griff. Have a good holiday,' the voice crackled back before signing off. He hooked the radio back up. Maddy frowned, surprised that he hadn't immediately contacted the next control area. But she had learned to fly in the busy airspace near London. Out here everything was more — well; relaxed.

'You're going on holiday?' she demanded. The words were out before she could recall them. She had assumed that he would be working, that she would at least have some time alone with Zoe to find out what was going on. But if he was going to be there all the time . . . He was staring at her. 'The air traffic controller said . . . ' she began, then coloured. 'It doesn't matter.'

'A couple of weeks' fishing, if you've no objection,' he said abruptly. He didn't elaborate and she left it. It didn't matter to her what he planned to do, and since she knew Zoe loathed fishing they would at least have some time alone to talk.

She glanced out of the cockpit. They had dropped height considerably, she noticed with surprise as they approached a small island. From the air it seemed deserted. Not a sign of life, no craft to mar the perfection of a narrow horseshoe inlet that ran up to a small, sheltered beach fringed with palms and tumbled rocks. There was no dwelling to spoil the perfect natural mop of lush greenery that decorated the hilltop centre although she knew that could be deceptive. Few islands were totally uninhabited and the windward side might be choc-a-bloc with holiday-makers. But somehow she didn't think so.

'Is that Paradise Island?'

'Like to have a closer look?' It wasn't a polite invitation and she turned at the sudden tenseness in his voice. Then the engine gave a little splutter and the propeller ceased to spin. Maddy watched, fascinated, as Griff switched off the engine, pushed in the throttle, turned off the fuel — classic textbook procedure prior to an emergency landing . . . 'Shoes, glasses, false teeth,' he snapped urgently. 'Open your door. Now!'

Her eyes saw what was happening but her brain wasn't taking any calls. 'I haven't got false . . . ' Then the sudden realisation that the engine had cut out, that the crackling chatter from the radio had abruptly ceased and that the only sound was the air rushing past the fuselage broke through the disbelief and she reacted. She kicked off her shoes, flung off her glasses, flipped the doorlock before burying her head in her lap.

2

Maddy, her head buried in her lap, waited for the impact and prayed. As they hit the water, there was a jolt that rattled her teeth and threw her against the restraints and she kept her hands tight about her head as they bounced across the smooth water of the inlet, biting down hard to stop a scream escaping. She was so tense that she didn't realise the plane had finally come to a halt until there was a touch on her shoulder. 'You can come out now, Miss Osborne.'

She lifted her head a little, hardly able to believe that they were riding on the glassy smooth water of the inlet. She knew enough to understand the skill it had taken to glide the little seaplane to a safe landing and she cleared her throat to tell him so. But when she tried to speak nothing came out. She cleared her throat again. 'Well, any landing you can walk away from . . . ' she said, somewhat flippantly, only to be surprised by the unexpected shake in her voice.

'In this case, swim away from.' They had come to a standstill in the middle of the bay. 'Or rather, paddle away from.' He glanced at her. 'At least you didn't have hysterics, for which small mercy I suppose I should be grateful.'

'I never have hysterics,' she said, but what had started as a rebuke degenerated into a nervous giggle that sounded stupidly loud in the utter silence of the inlet. 'Would now be a good time to start?' she asked.

'Why don't you save it until we reach dry land?' he suggested. 'Then you can really let yourself go.'

Griff opened the cockpit door on his side and climbed down onto the float, rocking the machine precariously. Maddy finally succumbed to a little scream and, terrified that the plane would tip over and sink, rapidly followed suit, slipping precariously as her legs buckled beneath her, unexpectedly all rubber. She clung for a moment to one of the wing struts, clenching her teeth to stop them chattering as, somewhat belatedly, she began to shake with the shocking realisation of just how close to catastrophe they had come.

Griff, however, was sitting astride the other float apparently quite unconcerned. Perhaps emergency landings were a regular occurrence for him and he took them in his stride. He turned and, seeing her clinging to the strut for dear life, raised a sardonic brow. 'What's the matter?'

'N-nothing.' It was suddenly quite ridiculously important not to appear a shivering wimp. 'I . . . I'm just not dressed for a swim, that's all.'

He turned and looked at her, a slight frown creasing his forehead. Then he shrugged. 'Strip off if you don't want your clothes to get wet,' he invited somewhat astringently. 'It won't bother me.'

She glared at him. 'I remember. You're impervious. Well, thanks all the same,' she replied with resolution, 'but I'm sure I'll manage. And I'm not about to do a limbo dance, either.' His eyebrows rose a touch and too late she remembered that, as her father had suggested, she was supposed to be the epitome of helplessness. 'Just in case you were wondering,' she added, and turned quickly away to stare down into water so clear that she could see the ripples of sand on the bottom. But that gave no indication of the likely depth — it could just as easily have been five feet or fifteen. And the beach was a couple of hundred yards away. Rather more than a paddle.

She lowered herself into the sea. As she'd suspected, it was too deep to stand. For a moment she hung onto the float, then she pushed off and headed towards the island, the desire for solid land, to feel the soft white sand of the beach beneath her feet suddenly quite overwhelmingly strong as her crisp, incisive crawl drove her through the water.

'Where are you going, Miss Osborne?' Griff's voice carried clearly across the surface of the sea and, surprised, she stopped and turned, treading water. Where on earth did he think she was going? He was still sitting astride the float, his strong, tanned thighs lapped by the wavelets.

'Sightseeing,' she snapped, and spluttered as the sea-water lapped into her mouth. 'Where do you think?'

'Haven't you forgotten something?'

Her only thought had been to get ashore. Despite the appearance of total isolation, there *had* to be someone about who could help them. 'What?' she demanded.

He pointed above his head. 'We can't leave this out here. When I said paddle, I meant paddle.' He demonstrated by dipping his hand in the water and using it like an oar to propel the aircraft forward.

'But . . . ' He was right, of course. The plane couldn't be left untethered in the middle of the bay. Even a gentle breeze could blow it out onto the reef, or onto the rocks that tumbled around the little bay, although right at that moment she was in no mood to care.

'But you're so *strong*, Griff,' she pointed out with just a touch of malice. 'You don't need little me to help you.'

His grin was heart-lurchingly unexpected. 'In this instance, Miss Osborne, strength has nothing to do with it. If I paddle on my own, I'll just go round in circles.' And he drew a small, insolent circle in the air with his hand. 'And since Paradise Island is uninhabited for most of the year our best hope of early rescue is if I can get the radio working.'

'Most of the year? What about now?' she asked hopefully. She found the thought of leaving him to paddle around in circles a tempting one.

'You're out of luck, I'm afraid. The owner doesn't have too much time for sunbathing.'

'And you would know?'

'Yes, I do.' She regarded him through

narrowed eyes. He might, of course, be bluffing. She was quite certain that he was capable of bending the truth to his own ends. But what ends? And his warning that they could not look for help from the island only confirmed her own impression from the air. The radio did seem to be their most likely hope of immediate rescue. And immediate rescue was very important. She hadn't the slightest wish to be stranded on a desert island with this particular man for a moment longer than she could help. If that meant helping him paddle his damned plane, then so be it.

She swam back to the plane and hauled herself onto the float she had so recently abandoned, but this time she had sea-water streaming from her hair and clothes.

'Pity about that,' Griff said, a little smugly, she thought as she wrung out her hair. 'You should have taken my suggestion. Wet clothes are so . . . uncomfortable.' She was painfully aware that her silk camisole was clinging revealingly

42

to her bare skin, that he could not fail to notice that she was not wearing a bra. He was enjoying her discomfiture; his sympathy, in fact, was pure mockery.

'They'll soon dry,' she snapped, although neither the top nor her fine linen calf-length shorts were likely to recover from their unscheduled drenching. 'Shall we get on?' she demanded, only too aware of his amusement and afraid that she had blushed once again. The afternoon sun drying the sea-water on her face made it difficult to tell.

Griff obligingly opened the float locker and, producing a couple of oars, tossed one across to her. She caught it, regarded it doubtfully, then following Griff's example she dipped it into the water and began to paddle. It took a few minutes to get the hang of it, and she was painfully aware that Griff was watching her floundering attempts at oarsmanship with amusement.

Maddy had to work twice as hard as he did to keep the plane going in a straight line, but she refused to beg him to take it more slowly. By the time they neared the beach the muscles in her arms, her back and legs felt as if they were on fire. As she lay weakly along the float, however, Griff jumped down into waist-deep water.

'We can push from here,' he said, then clicked his tongue against his teeth. 'Come along, Miss Osborne, there's no time to relax; we're not finished yet,' he said briskly, as out of breath as if he had just been for a gentle stroll along the beach.

Relax? But she didn't even have the strength to scowl. Instead she slid from the float and, ignoring her screaming muscles as best she could, helped him to ground the plane on the safety of the beach, then she simply fell back against the sand and closed her eyes. The sand was soft and blissfully warm, and she could have lain there for the rest of the afternoon, but Griff had other ideas.

'No time for sunbathing,' he advised. 'You'd better make a start collecting something to make a fire.'

'You're joking.' She didn't move. 'It's got to be eighty degrees.'

'I wasn't planning to sit by it and keep warm.'

'A signal fire?' Still she hadn't moved, but she opened her eyes, lifting her hand to shade them from the sun to look at her tormentor. He was standing ankle-deep in sand, muscular arms akimbo, regarding her recumbent body with irritation. Maddy, riled at this, said, 'How quaint. But wouldn't it be simpler to radio for help?'

'I don't expect you to understand, Miss Osborne, but the aircraft suffered a complete electrical failure. That's why we're in this predicament.'

'Can't you fix it?'

'I will certainly give it a try,' he conceded, 'but I'm a pilot, not an electrical engineer.' He shrugged. 'Of course, if you feel you are more qualified than me to check it out, I'd be quite happy to trade places.'

'I put a plug on a hairdryer,' she offered. 'Once.' Not quite the truth, but

45

she had very little insight into the workings of a radio.

'Then I'll leave you to start building a fire.'

Maddy eased herself into a sitting position, stifling a groan as every muscle protested. She had thought she was fit, but clearly her daily swim hadn't prepared her for the kind of punishment her body had just endured. 'Surely you carry flares?' she asked. 'Isn't it mandatory?'

He regarded her thoughtfully. 'Probably. I'll organise some next time I'm in dock.'

'I should have thought Dragonair would have insisted on it.'

'Dragonair?' He glanced up at the plane then offered a regretful smile. 'I'm afraid this old crate doesn't belong to Dragonair. I bought it from them a couple of months ago.'

'And they didn't bother to remove their logo? A little careless of them.'

'An oversight.'

'And in the meantime you're trading

on their good name . . . ' He regarded her with a wry smile, but Maddy wasn't interested in his shady trading practices. She had thought of something far more disturbing. 'That means . . . they won't be looking for you when you're overdue.'

'There's no reason why they should,' he agreed, apparently without concern. 'But I'm sure Zoe will raise the alarm, eventually. Meantime . . . '

'Firewood.' She glanced around. It was suddenly very important to start a fire. The small beach was thickly rimmed with palms that occasionally dropped storm-damaged fronds. It shouldn't be too much hard work to gather a few. 'Where do you want it?'

'Far enough away from the plane not to set light to it, wouldn't you say?' He grinned. 'Better keep that as a final resort.'

Maddy hauled herself to her feet and staggered up the beach. She had been flying in a pensioned-off crate flown by some ne'er-do-well pilot that her godmother had taken a fancy to. She threw him a sideways glance as he climbed into the cockpit. No. That wasn't fair. He was a first-class pilot. It was down to him that she was still in one piece.

And when she didn't arrive at the appointed hour Zoe would certainly raise the alarm. In fact, she thought with a sudden brightening of spirits, it was possible that a signal fire might bring help more quickly than Griff's attempts to repair the radio. This encouraging thought gave her all the incentive she needed and she moved more eagerly to gather palm fronds.

She was standing, hands on hips, admiring her handiwork when Griff joined her.

'Was that all you could manage?' He gave the structure a prod with his foot and her neat wigwam effect collapsed in an untidy heap. 'Well, it's a start, I suppose. You'll just have to put your back into it tomorrow.'

'A start . . . ?' she spluttered.

But he didn't give her a chance to tell him just how hard she'd been working. 'You can leave it for now. No one is going to be looking for us before morning and we've more urgent things to consider.'

'What could possibly be more urgent than a signal fire?'

His green eyes seemed to dance in the light reflected off the sea. 'Fresh water, food. And then there is the small matter of where we are going to spend the night,' he said. And he smiled.

'Spend the night?' she repeated dully. And suddenly the importance of what he'd said about the fire sank in. She would have to put her back into it tomorrow. Tomorrow!

In a sudden panic, she looked around and to her dismay saw from the angle of the sun that it was already well into the afternoon. Calm. She must keep calm. Easier said than done.

'Didn't you manage to fix the electrics?' she demanded. Then, realising that she sounded just a touch hysterical, she added as airily as she could manage with a throat that the very mention of fresh water had rendered a desert, 'Perhaps we'd better light the fire now.'

'That pathetic heap won't last long enough to attract attention,' he said dismissively.

'I'll fetch some more fuel,' Maddy said, and without waiting for his answer took a step towards the palms. He captured her wrist, halting her abruptly and preventing her from moving away. She tried to shake him off, be about her business. 'Let me go,' she demanded. 'I've got to — '

'Miss Osborne, right now it's more important that we prepare ourselves for the night.'

'I disagree,' she said.

'When I'm forming a committee I'll let you know. In the meantime, just do as you're told.' She tried to pull free, but made no impression on the firm grasp about her wrist and furiously opened her mouth to protest, but he wasn't interested. 'So, unless you can fish . . . ?'

'Fish? Of course I can't fish.'

'Well, since the island doesn't boast a local branch of Fortnum's one of us has to provide supper.' He glanced towards the tangled heap of palm fronds, a wicked glint lighting his eye. 'You could, of course, try sending a smoke signal . . . '

'Very funny.'

He shrugged. 'It's important, I find, to keep a sense of humour under even the most difficult circumstances.'

She glowered at him. 'Ha, ha.'

'That's the spirit. And tomorrow I'll teach you how to survive in the wild. If we're here long enough you might eventually catch something other than a cold — '

'Long enough!' she exclaimed.

He shrugged. 'I don't suppose it will be more than a day or two, Miss Osborne,' he said, and his mouth twisted into a dangerous little smile. 'You'll be home in time to unwrap the gifts heaped beneath your Christmas tree.'

'All I want for Christmas is a quiet holiday in the sun,' Maddy declared.

'Maybe.' He looked unconvinced. 'But we'll have to pass the time somehow.'

'In your dreams,' she snapped. His jaw tightened and this time when she wrenched on her wrist he did not detain her.

'There's a pool up there; I suggest you fetch some water.' Griff pointed to what might have been an overgrown path leading from the beach and held out a bucket that he had brought from the plane. In it were her sandals and a machete. In his other hand he carried a small fishing spear. 'A fair division of labour, don't you think? And, traditionally, fetching water is women's work.'

She ignored the bucket. 'You Tarzan, me Jane?'

He took her hand and placed the bucket handle in it. 'In your dreams, darling,' he murmured, with a grin that infuriated her far more than his words.

'Nightmare, more like,' she retaliated.

'How pleasant that we agree about something. And if you're back before me, light a fire,' he tossed over his shoulder as he turned away, apparently certain of her obedience.

'I haven't got a match,' she snapped. 'And, before you dare ask, I was never a boy scout!'

He turned then. His slow, appraising glance began at her feet and rose by way of a pair of long, willowy legs dusted with powdered white sand, the crumpled ruin of her shorts draped over well-rounded hips, a neat waist and the all too obvious curve of firm breasts unhampered by a bra under the damply revealing silk of her camisole. Then he met her eyes. 'Miss Osborne,' he said finally, 'I promise you that I would never, in a million years, mistake you for a boy scout.' He grinned as she gasped at his impudence, but, unabashed, he tossed her a lighter. 'Don't lose it,' he warned, 'or you'll be eating raw fish.'

'You've got to catch it first,' Maddy reminded him, before turning abruptly towards the dense green thicket at the edge of the beach. By the time she had reached it and stopped to put on her shoes, Griff had disappeared. For a crazy moment relief and panic in almost equal measure overwhelmed her, but panic was the marginally stronger feeling and she came close to chasing after him begging him not to leave her alone.

Oh, wouldn't he like that? she thought, deriding her own weakness. What ironical little twist of fate had stranded her on an uninhabited island with the most insolent, vexing man she had ever had the misfortune to meet? A vivid recollection of the way he had picked her up so effortlessly and swung her into the aircraft intruded uncomfortably. Vexing, perhaps, but dangerous too. She hadn't forgotten the unexpected jolt as his hands had grasped her waist, that long raking look that had burned into her soul.

Maddy felt a sharp stab of guilt. She

had angrily denied his accusation of flirting and yet she had found it hard to keep her eyes off him, and her reaction to his touch had hardly been discouraging . . .

'Oh, come along, Maddy,' she said firmly to herself. 'Zoe will be raising the alarm at this very moment.' And with that thought to comfort her she grasped the machete and with a savage swipe attacked the over-grown path. The eldritch screech of some unseen, unknown creature, caught up and echoed through the forest by a host of unearthly voices, almost undid her.

For a moment she stood rooted to the spot, heart pounding, her tongue like a lump of wood in her mouth, incapable of raising a cry for help. Then she saw the innocent agent of her terror flapping noisily high above her in the trees — a bird of some kind, brilliant blue, and then another and another. She began to laugh. Too many shocks for one day, that was all. That was all.

She sank onto her knees on the sand.

She was laughing, but there were tears rolling down her cheeks. She knew she was near hysteria and tried to fight it, dragging in air in a desperate fight for breath, but it was running away with her, unstoppable, until, without any warning, she was wrenched to her feet.

'Stop that!'

She tried to speak, to explain that she was trying to stop, wanted to stop, but she couldn't. Instead she continued to laugh uncontrollably, her tear-filled eyes rippling over Griff's angry image until his face swam before her. He shook her but that just seemed to make things worse, then unexpectedly he released her shoulder and slapped her.

Abruptly she stopped, her hand flying to her cheek, her head all too painfully clear in the sudden silence — clear enough to want to strike him back. But as her tawny eyes sparked a storm warning a long, shuddering sob shook her entire body and, with an impatient exclamation, Griff caught her in his arms, holding her against the broad strength of his chest while she shivered and fought him. 'Stop that,' he demanded harshly, then, a fraction more gently, 'Stop it, now.' Just as quickly as it had seized her, the hysteria left her and she stopped fighting, slumping against him, her cheek pressing against his warm shoulder, her head filled with the slow, comforting thump of his heartbeat. 'It will be all right,' he murmured. 'Trust me.'

Maddy raised long, damp lashes to look up into his face and for just a moment was certain the expression that darkened his eyes was concern. For a lingering moment she clung to that, needing to be held, comforted, then she gave a little gasp.

'I wouldn't trust you half as far as I could throw you,' she said, pulling abruptly away from the dangerous comfort of his broad chest, wiping away the shaming tears with the heel of her hand.

'I'll put your rudeness down to delayed reaction,' he said with a clipped, dismissive edge to his voice, and he released his hold on her and stepped back, leaving her swaying slightly on still unsteady legs. 'Just this once.'

That tone was all Maddy needed to stiffen her backbone, restore her to her senses. 'Were you waiting for me to thank you for such prompt intervention?' She raised her fingers tellingly to her cheek, stretching her jaw in a somewhat exaggerated fashion.

'No. But you have my assurance that you are entirely welcome, Miss Osborne.'

Her tawny gold eyes flashed angrily. ' 'Miss Osborne,' ' she mimicked. 'Such formality seems a little out of place in these surroundings. Particularly since I just gave you the opportunity to do what you've clearly been itching to do ever since you set eyes on me.'

She knew even as she said the words that she was being very stupid — stupid in a way that was quite unlike her — but the moment she had set eyes on this man she had recognised some

58

primeval attraction between them. He was regarding her now with a look that made her curl her toes as she fought the desire to lash out.

He reached out and captured a bright, wayward tendril of hair, wrapping it around his fingers and holding it up to the light. 'Red hair and a temper to match. A dangerous combination, Maddy Rufus,' he said, with that drawly, teasing voice that got right under her skin. She flushed, furiously, unaccountably angry with Zoe. Had she amused her young lover with the tale of how Maddy, furious at the bestowal of Rufus as a nickname because of her copper-red hair, had defiantly painted every strand of it scarlet? She whipped herself with the thought.

'I think, after all, that I prefer Miss Osborne,' she said coldly.

'You're quite sure about that?' He raised darkly defined brows in sardonic mockery.

She swallowed, hard. It was time to

take back some measure of control. 'Quite sure, Mr Griffin.'

He pulled his fingers from her hair, leaving a soft ringlet where they had been. But the moment of danger was over. 'I told you, everyone calls me Griff.'

Maddy, almost herself again, arched one darkly winged brow. 'Of course. 'Griff will do',' she said, not bothering to hide the edge of sarcasm. Then she gave a little shrug. 'Nothing wrong with it as far as it goes. Such a pity the same can't be said of the manners.'

Griff's mouth straightened in a mirthless smile. 'Let's be honest . . . Miss Osborne . . . you have a few failings in that direction yourself.' Before she could respond he handed her the bucket. 'Now, do you think we could resume this conversation some other time? It isn't going to stay light for much longer.'

* ★ *

For a while she took considerable satisfaction in imagining that each branch, each overhanging leathery leaf that she slashed in two with the machete bore the arrogant, overbearing, infuriating features of 'Griff will do'. The nerve of the man, to suggest that she was bad-mannered when he . . . But then she burst upon a scene so enchanting, so magical that it would have warmed the most cynical tour operator's heart and she instantly forgot her anger.

A shimmering cascade of water dominated the clearing, falling dizzyingly from some unseen source, tumbling and spilling out in tiny diversions to spray over moss-laden rocks and tropical ferns in a lacy mist before plunging into a large dark pool. Delicately patterned wild orchids trailed carelessly over the surrounding glade, epiphytes sprouted from the branches of trees that might have been there for a thousand years. A fairy scene from the Garden of Eden.

But if she had been Eve, Maddy thought with an unexpected giggle, and Griff had been Adam the human race would have had a bumpy start. *Oh, really?* Startled by this unexpected sideswipe from her subconscious, she found herself remembering all too vividly the feel of his arms about her. 'Really!' she said, out loud, as if this put the matter beyond doubt.

But the light was going under the eerie green canopy of the forest and she didn't have time to worry about her body's unexpected response to a man her head disliked quite intensely — or time to linger by the pool, strip off her clothes and wash away the salt and sweat that clung to her skin. Instead she scooped up a bucket of water and poured it over herself, gasping at the unexpected chill, then relishing the slow trickle of water through her hair, over her shoulders and down her body.

Tomorrow she would bathe here, she promised herself, dipping her hand into the pool, raising it to her lips to slake her thirst with the wonderfully clear water, before filling her bucket in much the same way as women have been doing since the beginning of history and making her dripping way back to the beach.

There was no sign of Griff, but Maddy had no need to be driven to build a cooking fire; she was hungrier than she had been since the beginning of her holiday. It didn't occur to her to doubt that he would succeed in the task he had set himself. Griff would succeed at anything he set his mind to. And just what has he set his mind to regarding you? her subconscious prompted. 'Nothing. He doesn't even like me,' she said, but couldn't help remembering that moment when he had looked at her, held her protectively . . . 'I'm immune,' she protested, shivering just a little. 'And besides, there's Zoe.' And, having cleared up that point, she set about making a fire.

When Griff returned with his catch she was coughing from the smoke that had blown in her face as the wind had eddied across the beach, waving her hand frantically to clear the air. He had stripped to the waist, his shoulders and chest were dewed with sea-water and his dark hair was slicked back. His shorts were still dry. Had he swum naked? She quickly dropped her eyes to the fire, glad that her cheeks were already pink from the heat, but if she had expected praise for her efforts she was doomed to disappointment.

'You were right about not being a boy scout,' was his only comment as, bare, sand-encrusted feet planted firmly apart, he stood over her and tossed a fish down beside her — for all the world, she thought furiously, like some caveman hunter bringing home the fruit of his labours. It was a grouper — a brown-mottled, bewhiskered fish, ugly as sin, but excellent to eat. This one was small for the breed. They could, Maddy knew, grow to positively monster proportions in the underwater caves where they lurked, but this one would make a good meal for the two of them. Griff had gutted and cleaned it, clearly assuming that she would take over the woman's role and do the rest.

She looked at it uncertainly. It wasn't that she couldn't cook. She poached a fine salmon when the occasion demanded, but cooking a grouper on an open fire without utensils had somehow been overlooked on her cordon bleu course.

Ignoring the fish, she scrambled to her feet and followed Griff in the direction of the plane. 'I'd like my bag,' she said stiffly, and waited for him to get it for her. 'I need a change of clothes.'

'Help yourself,' he said carelessly, taking the mooring rope and walking up the beach to the nearest palm, leaving her to pull her own heavy bag from the hold.

Maddy was achingly tired but she wasn't about to give this obnoxious creature the pleasure, the satisfaction of seeing that she was as near the end of her tether as she had ever been. She caught the handle and pulled furiously. The bag swung free rather more easily than she'd anticipated and she staggered back and sat abruptly on her backside with it in her lap. For a moment — one miserable, split-second moment as she sat on the wet sand — she wished that she really were one of those helpless, pathetic women who just cried when things got beyond them — the kind of woman whom men rushed to comfort at the drop of a hat, the kind of woman whom she was certain Griff would pick up, wrap in his strong arms and hug better. But she wasn't. She was a hard-working businesswoman who plastered her own cuts, and she reminded herself very firmly that she preferred it that way.

She scrambled quickly to her feet and searched for her sunglasses where she had thrown them on the floor of the aircraft. They weren't there and she climbed into the cockpit, finally spotting them poking out of the map pocket where Griff must have put them for safety. As she pulled them out an envelope came out with them, falling to the floor and spilling its contents — a cheque and a note.

She didn't mean to look but Zoe's familiar signature was unmistakable. And the sum made her gasp.

3

'Did you find what you were looking for?'

His voice, just below the cockpit window, made her jump and guiltily she pushed the cheque and note back into the envelope, stuffing them deep into the map pocket. 'Yes, thank you.' Forcing a smile to her lips, she turned and glanced down at him. 'Just my handbag.' She held it up.

'Your lipstick could certainly do with a retouch,' he agreed, but he held out his hands. 'Come on, I'll give you a hand down.' Surprised by this unlooked-for gallantry, she put her hands on his shoulders and allowed him to swing her to the ground. He held onto her waist for a moment longer than absolutely necessary. 'And if you want anything from the cockpit just ask me in future.'

Because she might see something

she shouldn't? Too late for that, Mr Griffin, she thought. 'I'm not entirely helpless,' she said stiffly, trying to ignore the the perilous nearness of his body. She didn't normally find it so hard. But then Hugo Griffin ignored every 'keep off' sign that she had erected with such care over the years . . .

'Whether you are helpless or not remains to be seen, but you won't be much use to me if you break your ankle, will you, Maddy Rufus?'

'I've no intention of breaking anything,' she snapped, but although his words were apparently callous, she knew he was right. It didn't make it any easier to take. He released her and returned to his task of tethering the plane and she found herself letting out a long, slow sigh of relief as she knelt and opened her bag to search for a T-shirt.

But Griff hadn't quite finished. 'I do realise that you wouldn't dream of sitting down to dinner without changing first,' he said, giving the rope a final tug. 'But since, for once in your life, you're going to have to cook it it might be advisable — '

'I wasn't actually planning on wearing an evening dress . . . ' she began, then saw amusement flicker momentarily in his eyes as they swept her damp, bedraggled figure before lighting on the elegant black gown that lay on top of her bag. 'At least, not this one. A little too formal for the beach.' She flicked it to one side. 'Now this . . . ' She held out a simple slip of a dress, cut on the bias from heavy cream silk.

His eyes snapped. 'I don't like you in that.'

Maddy stared at the dress. It was a favourite; she had been wearing it when Rupert had flung himself at her . . . Suddenly she didn't much care for it herself. 'No?' She dropped it and rose to her feet. 'I suppose it'll have to be the black, then.'

'I look forward to it. In the meantime your fire appears to have died down sufficiently to bake the fish.'

Her fire indeed! She laid no claim to it. 'And just how do you propose I do that?' she demanded. 'Or do you have a secret supply of aluminium foil?'

'No, but there's plenty of the local equivalent.'

'The local equivalent?' She propped her fists on her hips. 'I really can't wait to hear this.'

'Banana leaves.' He began to walk away, then stopped and turned back. 'Just watch out for the spiders.'

Maddy's scalp prickled. 'Couldn't you — ?' she began, then saw his slow smile.

'You're not scared, are you, Maddy? Only, you did say you weren't entirely helpless . . . '

'No, of course I'm not scared,' she said, too quickly, but in the face of his cool appraisal she clung stubbornly to her pride. 'I'm not in the least bit frightened of spiders.'

'No?'

Maddy disdained to answer but threw him a look that should have fried him on the spot. Disappointingly he appeared not to notice. In fact he walked away without so much as a scorch-mark.

It wasn't far to the spot where she had seen a banana tree and, knowing it would be fatal to stop and think, she immediately hacked off several of the thick, leathery leaves, leaping back as they crashed to the floor. Then she grabbed them by the tip and almost ran back to the beach, stumbling over roots as she went, her skin almost crawling as she flung the leaves from her and stepped quickly back, half expecting a host of hairy beasts to leap out and devour her. Nothing happened. Of course nothing happened. He had wound her up and she had performed, as obliging as a well-oiled clockwork toy.

'All right . . . Maddy?' Griff said lightly as he joined her, hardly bothering to hide his amusement.

'Just fine . . . Griff.'

'Now, while dinner bakes I suggest

you give a little thought to where you're going to build your shelter.' Startled, she looked up. 'You're more than welcome to share mine, of course,' he offered with mocking courtesy. 'But something tells me that you wouldn't be very keen on the idea.'

'Then you're more perceptive than I thought,' she replied, with considerably more poise than she was feeling, glad that the heat from the fire covered her blushes. 'I'd rather sleep on the beach.'

He smiled. At least, she thought that minute contraction of the lines fanning out from shaded eyes might just be his idea of a smile. 'Well, there's plenty of it to choose from. Help yourself,' he said provokingly.

Damn! She'd done it again — put his back up when he might have helped her. But she was not about to beg him to do anything for her if that was what he was hoping. Or was it worse than that? Was he taking advantage of the situation to make a little money from a wealthy young woman who was at the mercy of the elements? The thought was not a very pleasant one and, despite her father's suspicions, if she hadn't seen Zoe's cheque she was certain that it would never have crossed her mind. But now as she tried to push the idea away it seemed to take hold and grow. Well, there was only one way to find out.

She looked up at him, trying to ignore the strong line of his jaw, the blazing green eyes that promised so much . . . hypnotising her, enticing her into dangerous waters. 'How much would you want to build me a shelter?' she said abruptly.

'How much?' He said it lightly enough, yet his eyes had clouded and a muscle tightened at the corner of his mouth. 'It's odd but for a moment I almost believed you when you said you weren't entirely helpless.' He shook his head. 'There's no room service in paradise, Maddy. If you want a shelter you're going to have to build one yourself. I'm not for sale.'

Stunned, she remained motionless as he strode swiftly away from her. She should have been angry, but she wasn't Her heart was singing at his swift rejection of her offer of money. Then she came down to earth with a bump. With Zoe's cheque tucked away in his plane, he wasn't likely to risk everything for what she might offer.

'Damn! That wasn't very clever.' She glanced at the fire, but there was nothing left to do. 'Better change for dinner, Maddy, and put your thinking-cap on.'

At the far end of the beach the rocks formed a small enclosure, wide open to the sky but offering enough privacy to strip off and wipe herself down with the still damp flannel from her sponge bag before applying a generous helping of body lotion to her thirsty skin and brushing out her long copper hair. She applied insect repellent to the most sensitive areas and then dressed in a pair of thin cotton trousers and a long-sleeved T-shirt.

'You smell good enough to eat,' Griff remarked when she rejoined him. Maddy raised her eyebrows to cover her confusion at this unlooked-for compliment. 'I'm sure the bugs will be grateful for the invitation to dinner.'

'I'm wearing an insect repellent,' she replied, irritated with herself for falling into his trap.

'Really?' He regarded her thoughtfully. 'If I was an insect, I don't think I'd be repelled.'

'If you were an insect, I'd swat you,' she retaliated. It was his turn to raise a sardonic brow and it occurred to Maddy that if he were an insect, he would be a very large one and swatting him would not be so simple. 'Do you think the fish will be ready yet?' she asked quickly.

'No,' he said, and she had the uncomfortable feeling that he knew precisely the reason for her abrupt change of subject. What was it about him that set the hairs on her skin up like the fur of a cat rubbed the wrong way so that she constantly lashed out at him? His arrogant manner infuriated her, it was true, and she had concrete evidence that his interest in Zoe involved money in some way. They were reasons enough to dislike him, distrust him even, but that wasn't what bothered her. Her reaction to him was on a deeper, more unsettling level altogether. He had the kind of power that did something impossible to her insides whenever he was close. And, like iron filings near a magnet, she could find no way to escape.

As if to give the lie to this thought she moved away from him and threw herself down on the sand. But still her eyes were drawn irresistibly to him. The sinking sun lit his profile against the darkening rocks, glowing against the warm skin of his shoulders and chest. She shivered. There was something almost savage about him, as if this untouched wilderness was his perfect environment. And yet in the cockpit of his plane was Zoe's cheque. Civilisation with a vengeance.

A while later he tossed a couple of coconuts onto the sand beside her. 'I've no rum to make a punch, but it will help the fish down.'

'I prefer my coconut milk straight.'

'Just as well, under the circumstances.'

'But it's a bit rough on you,' she said with mock concern. 'You were going on holiday, weren't you?'

'Was I?'

'The traffic controller hoped you had a good time when you signed off.' He frowned and her heart gave an odd little lurch. Had she heard something she shouldn't? 'Were you going somewhere nice?' she asked, hoping she sounded a great deal more casual about it than she felt. Or had he been going somewhere with a numbered bank account where he stashed his ill-gotten gains? Was that why he had been so put out at having to come and fetch her?

He shrugged and stretched out on the sand beside her, propping himself on one elbow. 'Just a couple of weeks'

78

fishing. Here will do as well as anywhere.'

'You'll understand if I don't share your enthusiasm. I have absolutely no desire to spend two weeks here,' she said. His eyes danced over her face and she received the distant impression that she had said something to amuse him. But he didn't say anything. 'There isn't much in the way of home comforts or entertainment,' she reminded him.

'No, but I have you.'

'Me?' The word was startled from her.

'You are an endless source of entertainment, Maddy Rufus,' he said softly.

'I'm glad I prove useful for something.'

'Oh, you're going to be useful,' he assured her. 'Tomorrow you'll get your first fishing lesson. As for home comforts ... ' He waved a careless hand, taking in the scene around them. 'Perhaps you've been pampered long enough. It's time you had a taste of the *real* world.' Had she imagined the emphasis on 'real'? She certainly hadn't imagined the challenge in his voice, but she refused to apologise for her choice of holiday.

It was her first in the three hard years since she had started her own business. Spot a gap in the market and supply the need, was her father's philosophy, and never forget that people will always pay for the best. And after listening to his endless complaints about the poor quality of clerical staff available she had taken him at his word. But it had been hard work establishing her business and making it one of the most successful staff agencies in London. 'It looks,' she said somewhat pointedly, 'as if I'm going to have a taste whether I like it or not. At least until morning.'

'Well, don't worry. Paradise Island might be a little short on champagne but it has everything necessary for survival — good, clean water, fish to eat and fruit growing wild if you know where to look for it.'

'And coconuts,' she said, with just a touch of irony. 'Pity about the hot shower, a bed, and a well-stocked refrigerator.'

His eyes met hers. 'You don't need a refrigerator, there's a shower at the pool and if you want to sleep in comfort you could always weave yourself a hammock from wild vines.'

'Thanks, but I don't plan on stopping that long. The beach will do for tonight.'

'I do hope, for your sake, that the wind doesn't blow up.'

She picked up a handful of sand and let it trickle through her fingers. A windy night would be uncomfortable but she wasn't about to admit it. 'You've obviously been here before.' He didn't answer. 'When you've brought the owner here? Tell me about him. What's his name?' A thought suddenly struck her. 'Surely he has some kind of house here? Maybe even a radio?'

'Did you see any sign of a house?'

'Since I had my head in my lap I

didn't see much at all.' She shrugged. If there had been a house, a radio, he would have used it. 'Do you think Zoe might have raised the alarm by now?'

'Maybe.' He sounded doubtful. 'The trouble is, I didn't tell her precisely when to expect us. Just some time before dark.' He paused. 'Or, if I had something to drop off at one of the other islands, maybe tomorrow morning.'

Maddy stared at him, not wanting to believe it but knowing only too well that in the laid-back, easygoing atmosphere of the Caribbean it was all too possibly the truth.

'Tomorrow morning?' she said, very softly, scarcely trusting herself to say the words out loud.

'In fact I don't suppose she'll actually begin to worry until the evening. My schedule was a little hazy when I spoke to her this morning.'

For the first time since they had made their unscheduled and somewhat precipitate landing, Maddy felt like screaming

— just opening her mouth and screaming. But she didn't. It was far more important to find out just what he meant by 'hazy'. 'Did you say *tomorrow* evening?' she asked, with what she considered to be admirable self-control.

'That's not a problem, is it?' he drawled, with a stunning lack of concern.

'Problem?' She stared at him in total disbelief. 'Why on earth should that be a problem?' She didn't wait for him to answer but leapt to her feet and walked quickly down to the edge of the water. The sea swirled around her feet, sucking away the sand a little at a time, undermining her. Griff was doing that too — pulling away the certainties on which she had built her life, one by one: the certainty that she was firmly in control, the certainty that she knew exactly what she wanted, the certainty that she could never again feel anything . . .

⋆ ⋆ ⋆

'Time for dinner.' Griff's voice at her elbow a while later made her jump. He had piled a neat helping of the grouper's white flesh onto a piece of banana leaf and now offered it to her with mocking deference. The effect was somewhat sabotaged by his appearance. His shorts were oil-stained from his battle with the engine; he was wearing a fresh T-shirt, it was true, but the sleeves had been hacked from it without much consideration as to the aesthetics of the matter and his thick dark mop of hair looked as if it had been combed with his fingers.

'I'm not hungry,' she said, turning away, but he caught her chin and turned her back to face him so that the salty scent of the fish caught at the back of her throat.

'Of course you are. It won't hurt you to manage without cutlery and napkins for once.'

'I've eaten with my fingers before,' she said stiffly, lifting her chin away from his fingers.

'Really?' He sounded disbelieving. 'Don't worry, I won't tell. And the sea makes a pretty convenient finger-bowl.'

She gave him a cool glance, then shrugged and took the makeshift plate. 'Thank you,' she said, unbending slightly.

'You're very welcome.'

Maddy gave him a sharp look, but despite her suspicion that he was mocking her he appeared perfectly sincere. She settled back onto the sand and began to pull the fish to pieces with her fingers. Griff stretched out beside her and followed suit. She tried to ignore him, but short of turning her back to him that was impossible. And he would still be there. Probably until tomorrow evening. Better to try for some kind of truce.

'The last time I had grouper it was an enormous beast coated in rose mayonnaise, decorated with cucumber scales and with stuffed olives for eyes,' Maddy said, making an effort at neutral conversation but realising immediately that he would certainly take her words as a criticism of his efforts. She waited for Griff to make some disaparaging remark. He said nothing and somehow that was worse. Maddy felt her hackles rise. 'At a reception at the High Commission,' she added, forgetting her attempt at a truce in an effort to provoke him to some response.

Her father had business interests in the Caribbean and they had stayed in Barbados for a couple of days. Maddy, eager to get to Mustique had found it all rather irritating at the time, but the contrast between that event — the beautiful gowns of the women, the attentive, well-groomed young men eager to dance attendance on her every whim — and her present situation couldn't have been more spectacular.

'How did it taste?' he asked.

'Taste?' she asked absently.

'The fish?'

'Oh, the fish.' She considered the remains of her food. 'Not as good as this,' she admitted with some surprise.

'I don't suppose you'd worked as hard for it.'

She stiffened at the implied criticism. 'I certainly hadn't been in a plane wreck and hacked down half a jungle, if that's what you mean.'

'What else could I mean?' There was a teasing lilt to his voice and it was difficult to ignore the inviting way his eyes crinkled at the corners but Maddy did her best. 'You've the makings of a fine alfresco cook,' he said.

She had no wish to be thought a fine cook of any kind. 'I didn't do anything.'

'I've known women who could burn water,' he assured her.

'Really?' What women? How many? She slapped the errant thoughts away. 'Ah, well, there's a bit of a knack to water. I'm sure they had other talents that more than made up for it.'

He grinned. 'You may be right,' he said, and stood up, unfolding himself from the sand with the power and grace of a large cat. 'I think I'd better get the coconuts.'

Maddy bent to dip her hands into the sea to wash the fish from her fingers. The light was dying from a sky deepening rapidly from rose to purple. The swiftness of the Caribbean night never failed to startle or excite her. Already stars were appearing — glittering spots that would cluster and thicken in the intense darkness, so different from the pallid London sky that she was used to.

She turned as she heard Griff's feet on the sand behind her. He hefted a huge nut still encased in the thick green outer husk and with one swipe of the machete neatly sliced the top off. He handed it to her with a mock bow. 'I'm afraid you'll have to manage without a straw.' She pulled a face, then while he repeated the action with the second nut she tipped hers to her lips. Some of the milk made her mouth, most of it went down her chin.

'Next time I'll fly a scheduled airline,'

she spluttered, attempting to capture the drips in her palm. 'They carry such simple necessities as straws.'

'But they're so predictable, so boring.' He took the nut from her and hacked a chunk of husk away to make it easier to drink from.

'You mean they fly to a schedule and don't strand you on a desert island?' she said.

'Not without the statutory eight gramophone records to keep you entertained for the duration. And a packet of straws for the coconuts. Shall I sing to you?'

'That depends. How good are you?'

'I'm certainly the best baritone on this island.'

'You're the only baritone . . . ' He grinned. 'Why don't you sing 'Show me the way to go home'?' she suggested.

'London? In December? No, thanks.' He lay back on the sand, staring up at the stars, his hands linked behind his head. 'Most people dream of living like this, in paradise.

For the moment it's all yours. Why don't you relax and enjoy it while you can?'

'Relax? I've never worked so hard in my life.'

'But that's part of the pleasure. And this is the reward.' Above them the stars had clustered thickly, seeming almost close enough to touch against the velvet darkness of the night. She followed his example and lay back against the sand. 'Money can't buy this.'

'Easy for you to say. I'll bet whoever owns this island would tell a different tale.'

'You really shouldn't judge other people by your own standards.'

'At least I have some . . . ' A shooting star streaked across the sky but before she could say anything Griff had seized her hand.

'Don't waste your wish, Maddy,' he warned. 'You'll be rescued soon enough.'

'I've nothing else to wish for.'

'Nothing?' Griff demanded, rolling over and propping himself upon his elbow. For a moment he stared down at her, a small crease furrowing his brow. 'I think that's the saddest thing I've ever heard.'

'Nonsense,' she said a little defensively. 'What's sad about it? I've everything that I could ever want.'

'Everything?' His frown deepened. 'You're a healthy young woman. Have you no desire for a family of your own?'

'How typical,' she declared, sitting up abruptly, and, pulling her hand free, she hugged her knees. The question was too personal, too intimate; it touched a raw and empty place within her. 'How typical of a man to believe that all any woman wants from life is a chance to wash his socks.'

'I doubt you'll ever have to wash anyone's socks,' he said with just a touch of sarcasm.

'The socks were metaphorical,' she said crushingly. 'It's the attitude — ' She broke off, rather afraid that the small sound that had escaped his lips might have been stifled laughter. 'Besides,

I have to find the right man first.'

'One with metaphorical feet, presumably.' He turned away and began to pick up small shells and toss them into the sea. 'What was the matter with the guy you turned down the other night?'

'You wouldn't understand,' she said.

'You could try me. We've nothing else to talk about.'

'We could talk about you for a change. What brought you to the Caribbean, for instance?'

'A job. The chance to do what I love most.'

'Flying? Don't you miss home?'

He turned to her. 'This is my home.'

'But you're English.'

'I've nothing to go back to Britain for. My father died in a mining accident when I was seven, my mother worked herself to death to give me an education — ' He stopped abruptly. 'You're not getting off that lightly. You've a wish to make.'

She felt she had touched something, come close to what drove Hugo Griffin.

But his face was shuttered and barred. 'There is something,' she admitted. 'I wish I had a cup of tea.'

He threw back his head and laughed. 'Make it a pot, I'd enjoy a cup, as well.'

'It's my wish,' she said primly, then stretched back on the sand and closed her eyes. 'If you want a cup of tea, you must wish for one yourself.'

'You'd enjoy it more if you shared,' he advised her, making her feel rather small. 'Besides, I've already made my wish.' This unexpected admission startled her into opening her eyes. He had rolled onto his stomach and was looking down at her, staring most particularly at her mouth, and her lips began to throb in time with her heartbeat.

'What?'

'If I tell you what it is, it won't come true. But I promise you I didn't waste it on a cup of tea.' His voice was velvet-rich and, to Maddy's ears, heavy with meaning. For a dangerous moment she was certain that he intended to kiss her and for a dangerous moment she wanted

93

him to do just that.

'You mustn't wish for money,' she said quickly, with just a touch of panic in her voice. 'It has to be something totally impossible. A dream . . . '

'I know the rules and I'm very much afraid I've complied with every one.'

'An impossible dream?'

' 'If ever any beauty I did see / Which I desir'd and got, t'was but a dreame of — ' ' He stopped abruptly, but Maddy didn't notice. She had seen something out of the corner of her eye and leapt to her feet, showering him with sand, oblivious to his furious exclamation.

'The fire,' she said. 'We've got to light the fire.' Without thinking she grabbed his hand. 'There! Look, a light . . . '

'It's very faint.'

Barely there at all. A tiny light that came and went with the motion of sea. It was probably miles away. 'But it might be a yacht!'

'It might just be a fisherman in a dinghy. Whatever it is, it's a long way away, Maddy,' he warned.

'But if we can see them they must be able to see us.'

'Only if they're looking.' Still he hadn't moved and time was passing.

'We have to try!' she insisted, groping in her pockets. 'Where's the lighter?'

'You used it to light the fire.' He was right but she didn't have it now. Had she dropped it? Her heart was beating too fast. Too fast to think clearly. Why wasn't he doing anything? 'Did you leave it in your shorts?' Had she? She threw a panic-stricken glance out to sea. Was the light still there? She searched frantically for a moment and then saw it once more. Further away?

Ignoring Griff's sharp exclamation, the jab of pain as her foot snagged against a shell half-buried in the sand, she turned and pounded along the beach to the pale smudge where her shorts were draped over a rock to dry.

For a moment her fumbling fingers missed the cheap little plastic throw-away tube that might save them and she was certain that the only means of signalling her presence on the island was lost somewhere in the sand. Then her fingers closed about the lighter and relief surged headily through her veins.

'Found it?' She hadn't heard Griff come up behind her and she jumped, quite literally, and for a moment the lighter wobbled precariously. His hand closed about her fingers, steadying them. 'Give it to me.'

He gathered the sprawled heap of palm fronds, scattered where he had kicked at the heap she had so neatly arranged, and Maddy fumed at the delay as he gathered a few pieces, broke them up to make kindling. Then she heard the snap of the lighter. There was a spark, but no flame.

'Come on,' Maddy urged.

'The lighter's wet,' he said, trying again.

'Let me try,' Maddy demanded impatiently. 'I did it before.'

He looked up, staring out to sea for a moment before handing over the lighter. She clicked it and it immediately burst into a bright flame but her shaking fingers couldn't make the kindling catch.

'Leave it, Maddy.' Griff's voice was gentle. Too gentle. He touched her shoulder. 'Whatever was out there has gone.' She refused to give up. 'The light has gone,' he repeated, then sank down onto his heels beside her and caught her hand, taking the lighter from her. Then he put his arm about her and pulled her to her feet, leaving the dark sea to confirm what he'd said.

She stared beyond him, scouring the surface of the water, determined that he should be wrong. But only starlight silvered the tips of the gentle waves.

'Oh.' The word was a little gasp as she realised just how much her hopes had leapt at the possibility of rescue. 'I'll organise everything better tomorrow. If only the lighter hadn't been wet . . . ' She frowned. 'It worked when I lit the cooking fire.'

'These throw-away jobs can be temperamental.'

'I suppose so. And it doesn't matter,'

she said, lifting her chin a little to hide her disappointment. 'We'll be missed sooner or . . . ' The gentle hiccup of a sob broke through her brave words and somehow, before she knew what had happened, she was enfolded in a pair of strong arms and held against Griff's shoulder, his fingers tangling in her hair as he attempted to comfort her. And, heaven knew, she wanted to be held and comforted.

'Not quite as hardbitten as you thought?' he murmured, but she shook her head. He didn't understand. She was very far from being hardbitten, and right now the desperate see-sawing of her emotions had left her quite beaten. 'You're tired, Maddy. Come on. You should try and get some sleep.'

'Sleep?' The impossibility of sleeping under such circumstances appeared to have escaped him. But she didn't argue, allowing herself to be half led, half carried up the beach to the little lean-to hut he had built.

She was oddly reluctant to let go of

him. It was dark and the little noises of the Caribbean night reached out from the forest, the ardent call of a bullfrog overlaying the stridulations of a million tiny creatures that from the fortified, nature-defying terrace of the Mustique beach house would have sounded charming. Here everything was so much closer, and as he set her down on the sand she clutched at him. 'Don't leave me.'

'I'm not going anywhere,' he said a little wryly as he detached her hands from his shoulders. 'Go on now. Go to sleep.'

She slid beneath the dark thatch of the makeshift hut and curled up into a defensive little ball like a miserable child. He had laid something — a towel, perhaps — over the sand. To her weary limbs it felt as soft as a feather bed. For a moment she lay there, conscious of tears welling in her eyes as she wondered whether her father was safely home. He would phone Zoe, expecting to speak to her. What would

Zoe tell him? Then her brief descent into self-pity filled her with disgust and she rubbed angrily at her wet cheeks. She never cried. Griff was right — she should try and get some sleep. Everything would seem better in the morning.

Maddy eased off her trousers and rolled them up to make a pillow and then stretched out. Tomorrow they would be rescued and all this would just seem like a dream, she decided as she was caught out by an unexpected yawn. A very bad dream. Then she closed her eyes.

★ ★ ★

Maddy woke to a brilliant light shining in her eyes. And she blinked, trying to think where she was and why the bed was so hard. Then as she half turned to ease herself one thing became startlingly apparent. She was not alone.

4

Paradise. She was in paradise and Griff's smoothly muscled arm was about her waist, holding her fast against the warm, comforting frame of his body. She had asked him not to leave her and he had taken her at her word.

And shining in at her was the moon, huge and white, lighting a white path across the inlet as it sank slowly into the sea. For a moment Maddy watched entranced, the curve of her back nestled against his chest, her long legs tangled with his, which were longer still and shockingly hair-roughened.

For a moment she lay there, surprised by the rush of warmth, the unexpected pleasure of lying tucked within the protective curve of his body. Then his hand moved gently over her stomach to cradle the soft swell of her breast and Maddy froze. He had

101

assumed her mute acceptance of his presence meant something else. In a moment of weakness last night she had wanted comfort, needed comfort But not that kind. She erupted from his grasp, leaping up without a thought as to the consequences.

'What on earth . . . ?' He swore volubly as palm fronds showered down on him, the lean-to disintegrating about his ears. 'What the hell are you playing at?' he demanded, leaping to his feet and turning on her.

'Nothing. I have no desire to play.'

'And you think I have. Don't flatter yourself, woman,' he retorted, flinging off a palm leaf that clung stubbornly to his back. 'You were the one who begged me to stay with you; I was just — '

'Just what? Helping yourself?'

'If I had any intentions of helping myself, do you think you'd be talking about it right now? I *don't* help myself — '

'Oh, really? Well, I suggest you remind your roving hands,' she threw at him. 'They're not quite so restrained.'

For a moment he stared at her. 'My roving hands?' He said the words slowly, deliberately and took a step towards her. Maddy took a nervous step back. 'Where did they rove, Maddy?' She took another step back from eyes blazing darkly in the moonlight.

'I . . . I don't want to talk about it,' she snapped.

'Oh, but I insist. I want to know what fantasy has been conjured up by that overheated imagination of yours.'

'No fantasy,' she declared hotly, and this time as she stepped back she felt the sand wet beneath her feet.

'You don't imagine I was going to . . . take advantage of you, do you?' Maddy was beginning to regret her somewhat precipitate reaction. No doubt Griff had simply taken what had seemed to him the obvious and sensible decision to sleep alongside her, and if she didn't object to taking it further — well, she was certain that, despite his protestations, he would be more than happy to oblige. Or maybe he thought that she would willingly accept the situation in return for his protection. He seemed to have a pretty low opinion of her generally . . . 'Well?' he demanded. He was in front of her now, stripped to the waist, his powerful shoulders and broad chest far too close.

'You were half-asleep,' she said placatingly, retreating again into the water. 'It doesn't matter. Leave it. Just . . . oh, just go away,' she said helplessly, putting out a hand to fend him off.

'I'm going nowhere, and neither are you, Maddy Osborne. And I think it's about time you learned a few manners.'

The water was well up around her calves now. 'There's nothing wrong with my manners. You're the one who should learn to — ' He didn't wait to discover what she thought he should learn. Instead he plunged forward and grabbed her arms and she let out a startled little scream.

He grinned. She saw the white gleam

of his teeth and wondered how anyone quite so objectionable had managed to keep them for so long. 'Come on,' he taunted. 'You can do better than that. Or are you waiting for me to give you something to really scream about?'

'You already have,' she replied, perhaps unwisely, because he stepped a little closer and without warning shifted his grip to her waist.

'Oh, no, Maddy Rufus. You really can't expect to get off that lightly. I'm not one of your pet playboys to be twisted around your little finger then humiliated for your amusement.'

'I didn't — ' But as he jerked her body close to his there was no time to explain. 'What are you going to do?' she gasped.

'I wonder what it would really take to make you scream as if you meant it,' he drawled, with a voice like velvet being shredded very slowly. 'Just a kiss, perhaps?' Maddy stood very still, steeling herself for the ordeal, her mind flashing a warning to her treacherous body that even now, as the cooling sea swirled around her thighs, was beginning to pound with her overactive heartbeat.

'No — ' But her protest was cut off as his lips brushed hers as delicately as if he had touched them with the curved petals of a hibiscus. It sent a tiny tremor winging through her body like a thousand panicking butterflies. His hands were no longer hard upon her waist. They still held her, but lightly, drawing her traitorously willing body closer until her thighs were pressed against his legs. She was wearing only a pair of the most delicate silk pants, a T-shirt that clung revealingly to betray the eager thrust of her breasts, but she made no move to pull away. 'Griff . . . ' she pleaded, but had no idea what it was she wanted.

'No scream that time, Maddy Rufus,' he said, his breath as soft as down against her cheek. 'I'll have to try harder.'

The muscles in her stomach contracted as she sensed a more demanding edge to his voice. 'No!' This time her protest was more urgent as she came to her senses and began to struggle. This wasn't her. She didn't . . . But as she flung a fist at his shoulder he bent and caught her behind the knees, swinging her up into his arms. 'Let me go! You can't . . . you mustn't . . . ' For a long moment he looked down at her, his dark eyes challenging her to prove that she meant what she said. Too long. She suddenly realised that she had ceased to struggle and was lying back in his arms, no longer sure of anything. 'Let me go!'

His mouth curved into the most sensuous of smiles. 'Now?' he asked, very softly, and without waiting for her reply he did as she asked.

It was as if she fell in slow motion, hitting the sea with a splash that sent streams of phosphorescent water rising high above her in a bright arc. It almost seemed to Maddy that she could count every drop as it fell back to the sea before everything went momentarily black then white as she was submerged in the maelstrom of water churned up by her struggle to right herself.

After a moment she found her feet and burst from the surface, waist-deep, gasping with shock blazing with indignation, and this time there was no mistake about the scream. Uncontainable fury, all the repressed emotion of a terrible day, sheer outrage at the cavalier way she was being treated by this arrogant monster of a man rent the air and found a sympathetic echo in a flock of startled birds who flapped and shrieked at being disturbed so early from their roost.

Griff was standing, arms akimbo head thrown back, laughing with undisguised delight at the mayhem he had caused. 'Now, that scream,' he said, shaking his head, 'was very convincing. I suggest you remember it for future use.' Then he flipped the button on his shorts and Maddy backed rapidly away.

'What — what are you doing?' she spluttered.

'I'm going for a swim. You can join me if you like.'

She blushed fiercely as the pre-dawn light glistened on the hard planes of his magnificent naked body as he turned away and tossed his shorts onto the beach. 'Not if you were the last man on earth,' she retorted indignantly.

He grinned at her. 'Better hope you're rescued soon, then.'

'I'll make certain of it!'

But despite her angry words she couldn't stop herself from turning back to watch him as he powered away across the water in a fast overarm crawl. The pre-dawn light was enough for her to have determined that his glistening body was all one colour, confirming her suspicion that he was a stranger to a swimsuit. And, alone in paradise, who needed one?

Except that right now he wasn't alone.

He really was the most infuriating man she had ever met. She raised her fingers to her lips and discovered that despite everything she was smiling. Infuriating he might be, but it could not be denied that he was a great deal more invigorating than the likes of poor Rupert Hartnoll. She caught herself. And a great deal more dangerous. If she wasn't careful she would still be standing there when he returned to the beach. That thought alone was enough to make her move. Fast.

★　★　★

Maddy rescued her trousers from the wreckage of Griff's hut, shook out the sand and folded them neatly. She did the same for the towel. It was blue — a very large and expensively thick American plush towel. The kind that Zoe loved. She dropped it quickly and stepped back. Then she turned and ran.

Her bag was in the hold of the aircraft and she wasted no time in sorting out some fresh clothes for what would undoubtedly be another difficult day. She pulled out a tiny white bikini, then hurriedly replaced it with a more decorous one-piece bathing suit in her favourite dark mossy-green. It would be madness to be unnecessarily provocative.

She added a baggy white T-shirt, picked up her sponge bag and towel and as the sky turned pink with the rising sun, headed up the path to the pool for the bathe she had promised herself.

It was strange climbing up the empty path with only the chattering of birds and insects to disturb the silence. She might have been the first person in the world. Even as the thought entered her head she turned nervously. There was no sign of Griff, but she wasn't alone and the thought that he wouldn't swim forever spurred her on.

The pool was, if possible, even more beautiful in the early-morning light. A delicate mist was drifting off the water and curling over the lush vegetation, wrapping itself around the trailing orchids and morning glory vines already beginning to unravel their vivid blue flowers to the first early rays of the sun.

Maddy made her way to the side of the pool where the flying spray had been diverted to miss the pool and fly off onto a flat slab of rock, providing a natural shower — the work of the absent owner presumably. But whoever had done it she was grateful. She stripped off and stepped beneath it, gasping at the sudden chill on her warm skin. But after a few moments she quickly became used to the temperature and turned to a nearby rock to reach for her shampoo. As she did so, a particularly piercing wolf-whistle rent the air.

Furiously, Maddy grabbed for her towel. Holding it in front of her and sweeping her streaming hair from her face, she turned to confront her tormentor and tell him exactly what she thought of him. But Griff wasn't to be seen. She frowned. Griff was no voyeur, she thought edgily. He was far more likely to have stripped off and joined her under the shower. And this thought made the fine hairs on the back of her neck rise and her skin prickle nervously. Because if Griff wasn't whistling at her, then who was?

'Griff?' Maddy called uncertainly.

'Griff?' The word was echoed mockingly back at her, perfectly catching the hesitant inflection of her voice.

'Griff! Stop it! she said abruptly, and took a step forward. 'It's not funny.'

'What isn't funny?' Griff asked as he appeared on the path below her. Seawater glistened on hard shoulders and the sculpted muscles of a chest scattered with dark hairs that curled lazily down his taut belly and disappeared beneath the towel tied carelessly about his loins. She jerked her eyes away, certain that he was wearing nothing else.

'*You* aren't,' she snapped, clutching her own towel tightly before her, glad of the dim light to cover her blushes. Anyone would think that she had never seen a man before — and in the briefest of swimsuits that were far more revealing than his towel. But not, she was forced to admit, a man like this. She shook herself angrily. A beautiful body meant nothing if the spirit was corrupt — she knew that. No one better.

Griff raked his fingers through the tousled, sun-kissed warmth of his dark brown hair turned momentarily black by the deep shadows. 'You've lost me, lady,' he said. 'But if you've finished with the shower . . . ?'

'No, I haven't as well you know.' She made a grab for the shampoo bottle but it slipped through her wet fingers and fell with a splash into the pool. Unable to reach for it without exposing her naked rear for his amused inspection, she watched helplessly as, driven by the spray from the falls, it bobbed out of reach. 'Could you pass that to me?' she asked stiffly, aware, despite his perfectly straight face that he was deriving considerable amusement from her predicament.

'I could,' he said, but made no move to help.

'Please,' she added, a little belatedly.

'You're learning, Maddy Rufus,' he said, with an insolent little smile that sent shivers dancing along her spine, before reaching out to fish the plastic bottle from the water. But he didn't immediately surrender it. Instead he opened it and poured a little into the palm of his hand. 'Smells expensive.'

'It's just ordinary shampoo.' She held out her hand.

'Turn around; I'll wash your hair for you.'

'No,' she said, spotting the quizzical glint in his eyes too late. She took a deep breath. 'I can manage. If you will just pass me the bottle.'

'It's no bother at all,' he assured her, moving easily towards her, and she backed nervously under the shower. 'And while I'm doing it you can tell me what didn't make you laugh.' In Griff's distracting presence, she had forgotten about the wolf-whistle, but he didn't give her an opportunity to remonstrate with him; instead he put a hand on her shoulder and turned her round to face the water before whipping the towel away. 'You don't want it to get wet, do you?' he asked with all seriousness as she made a frantic grab in an attempt to keep it, and he tossed it out of reach so that she was left with no means to cover herself, apart from her arms.

She employed them swiftly and strategically and keeping her back turned firmly towards him, spat fiercely, 'Go away!'

He took no notice and she fumed, trapped and helpless, as he stroked the shampoo down the length of her hair. 'Your hair is a beautiful colour, Maddy,' he said. 'Like a skein of copper silk Have you ever been to New England in the fall?' he asked conversationally, apparently unaffected by the fact that the hairs on his chest were brushing against her shoulder-blades, raising goose-flesh in a way that the chilly water had failed to do.

Maddy tried to speak but found that she had to clear her throat and concentrate very hard before she could answer. 'No,' she said, a little hoarsely.

'The trees have just this tint. Are you cold?' he asked with every appearance of concern. She was shaking, but not with the cold, and she was convinced that he knew that it was the touch of his fingers working slowly over her scalp, the pads of his thumbs pressed lightly against her temples, that was sending the shivery sensation to every nerve-ending. But she didn't have to make a complete fool of herself and admit it.

'Yes,' she said, crossing her fingers hard. 'The water's freezing.'

'You'll get used to it. And cold showers are good for the soul.'

'Have you rinsed out all the soap?'

'Not quite.' And he seemed in no hurry to end her torment, no matter what the cause. Instead, he lifted her hair through his hands, offering it to the spray. 'Quite beautiful.'

'I thought perhaps you didn't like redheads,' she said, not wishing to hear his smooth compliments.

'Really? Just because I haven't joined the army of admirers willing to fall in homage at your feet? Are you conceited as well as unkind?'

'Unkind?' She half turned, then, remembering, quickly turned back to the shower. 'If you're referring to that idiotic scene with Rupert, I apologised to him.'

'I would have thought that took a bit of doing.' As Maddy jerked angrily away from him she found herself hauled back by her hair, which had somehow become entangled in his fingers. 'The colour is immaterial,' he continued, apparently oblivious to her outburst. 'I just like hair to be long and shiny.' A long, raucous wolf-whistle echoed that sentiment and Maddy swung her head round to stare at Griff.

'It wasn't you!' she exclaimed.

'What?'

'The wolf-whistle.'

'Was that why you were all steamed up?' he asked.

'I thought you were playing a rather

118

nasty joke,' she said indignantly. 'Trying to frighten me.'

'Not my style, lady.' He turned and looked up into the trees and then gave a lazy whistle. A small brown parrot, with pale blue head-feathers and a bold flash of yellow and orange on his wing, flapped down from the canopy and alighted on a nearby rock. The bird put his head on one side and peered at her with bright, beady eyes. 'Maddy,' Griff said, 'meet Jack. Jack, say, How d'you do?'

'How d'you do?' the parrot obediently repeated.

Maddy gave an uncertain little laugh. 'He's tame.'

'No. He was once, but he must have escaped from a passing yacht, or a nearby island. He's a St Vincent, so someone local probably owned him. He comes when he's whistled; he enjoys human company.'

'He's lovely. But he must be lonely, or does he have a mate?'

'No, he's quite alone. Freedom

always has a price. And he's no lonelier than he was fastened to someone else's perch.'

'The perch has certain advantages.'

'An endless supply of sunflower seeds? A life of ease? Well, you should know. You live in a gilded cage. Jack and I have other ideas.' She was going to protest, tell him indignantly that he didn't know what he was talking about, but he had already turned away to retrieve her towel. He wrapped it around her, tucking it in firmly at the back, and as his knuckles grazed her shoulder-blades her tongue seemed to have momentarily turned to wood.

She turned and looked up at him and for a moment he met her gaze head-on, his eyes, ocean-deep, daring her to challenge him and take the consequences, and for a moment she confronted him, taking on the razor-edged scorn. She'd done it countless times. She had no trouble facing down men who thought a woman in business was an easy target, men who refused to accept that she had no desire to indulge in a little meaningless sex.

But Griff made her feel vulnerable, uncertain and she faltered under that sharp, unwavering focus and finally dropped her eyes.

'Can you spare a little of your ordinary shampoo?' he asked, apparently careless of the fact that her heart was beating like a power-hammer. She wanted to tell him to go to hell in a handcart, but he was already reaching for the towel that snaked about his hips.

'Help yourself,' she said, snatching up her clothes. And she fled.

Back on the beach she quickly donned her swimsuit and applied sun block to every exposed inch, before covering herself with a baggy white T-shirt that came almost to her knees. Then, firmly ignoring her stomach's demand for breakfast, she began the earnest task of building the largest signal fire she could manage. It had suddenly become very important that she get back to civilisation.

Griff reappeared after a while, carrying what looked impossibly like a pineapple. But she studiously ignored him, intently ferrying back and forth across the beach to add to her pile of debris. When she was satisfied she collected the machete and began to hack some of the green fronds from a palm that overhung the beach.

'What are you doing?' Griff interrupted the shredding of a coconut with a clasp-knife to enquire.

'I'll need some green stuff to make smoke.'

'Oh, serious stuff,' he said with a grin.

'You could help.'

'I could. Except, of course, that I'm not in your desperate hurry to return to civilisation.' She refused his invitation to spar. 'Well, you'd better come and have some breakfast or you'll faint before assistance arrives.' Maddy was already beginning to feel a bit light-headed and didn't argue. 'And you should be wearing a hat.'

'The maid at the villa fell in love with mine so I gave it to her. I was going to buy a new one on Palm.'

'That's a pity. If you get sunstroke, who'll build the fire and fetch the water?'

'It's possible that you might have to do it all by yourself.'

He laughed, deep lines biting into his cheeks — the white flash of teeth, the sheer unexpectedness of it leaving her completely unguarded. 'Here, try this.'

He had cut a coconut in half to provide them each with a bowl and into it he had piled the shredded flesh of the nut and some pineapple, moistening the mixture with the coconut milk.

'This is delicious,' she said, scooping it up with her fingers. 'You have the makings of a fine al fresco cook.' She met his glance without flinching and felt quite proud of herself. 'Is it fish for lunch?' she continued, pushing her luck.

'Unless you can think of anything more original.'

123

'I don't have time to think. I have a bonfire to light. Has the lighter dried out, or am I reduced to rubbing two sticks together?'

'Don't tempt me!' He glanced at the sea. 'Hadn't you better wait for a boat or something to signal to?'

'Like last night?' she demanded, with a warning flash from her eyes. 'I plan to keep the fire going all day if necessary. That way I won't miss anything.'

'Then you'll be kippered by tonight,' he said with a careless shrug as he tossed her the lighter and turned to walk away.

'You could stay and give me a hand,' she pointed out. 'Unless you've something more important to do?'

'I'm on holiday, remember. Besides, I can't bear to watch a woman work.'

'Then don't stick around or you're likely to faint dead away from the shock.' She nodded in the direction of the plane. 'You could always have another go at the radio.'

'Indeed I could.' And he smiled as if

something had greatly amused him. It did something impossible to his face, deepening the lines carved into his cheeks, straightening the sensuous curve of his mouth, and it made his pirate's eyes sparkle like the ocean in the early-morning sun. It was an almost irresistible combination. Maddy turned abruptly away before she succumbed and returned his smile, but as she bent to light her signal blaze she discovered that it required two hands to keep the lighter steady.

Drat the man, she thought crossly as the dry kindling began to burn and she settled back on her heels. If he really disliked her so much, why wouldn't he help with her attempts to signal for rescue instead of wasting his time messing about with a radio that he had already admitted he couldn't fix? Surely he had no more wish to be stuck with her company than she wished to be inflicted with his?

She twisted her head to glance back over her shoulder. Griff was sitting in the cockpit, the radio receiver in his hand and for a moment her heart leapt in dizzy expectation that he had managed to bring it to life. Then as he saw her looking he idly waved a screwdriver in her direction.

She turned sharply away and gave the fire a poke with a large stick. Sparks flew upwards as a sudden draught from the sea whipped it into life, and within minutes a satisfactory column of smoke was rising from the slower-burning sappy leaves. Maddy, well pleased with her efforts, sat back to scan the horizon. But for an area where the sea was a way of life for the local people as well as a haven for holiday-makers it was oddly empty. She had hardly expected to attract the attention of one of the liners that carried the tourists from island to island. But there was not one yacht, not one tiny fishing boat.

'You've made a pretty good job of that,' Griff said, a few minutes later, coming to rest on his haunches alongside her, his knee perilously close to hers.

'It's just a pity there's no one to see it.'

He gave her a sideways glance. 'Did you expect a major search to be under way for you by now? Fleets of boats searching for wreckage? Aircraft scouring the sea? Newsmen pouring in from the four corners of the earth to cover the story?'

Maddy was temporarily lost for words. 'Why on earth would the Press be interested?'

'It will surely cause a ripple of excitement if it becomes known that the daughter of one of Britain's most wealthy entrepreneurs is missing?'

'Perhaps,' she conceded, a little uneasily. 'But because of your lackadaisical attitude to schedules apparently even Zoe hasn't yet woken up to the fact that I'm more than half a day overdue.'

'But she will,' he replied evenly. 'Eventually.' If he noticed her furious scowl he didn't let it show. 'Meanwhile,' he continued, 'since you aren't hurt and you aren't about to starve, why don't you just relax and discover the simple pleasures of life? It's surprising what fun you can have without resorting to the bottomless credit card.'

'Enjoy myself! How can I?' She jabbed furiously at the sand with her stick. Griff reached across and took it from her, his long fingers brushing against the back of her hand, to send a tiny quiver of excitement through her. She glanced sideways from under lowered lashes at Griff's powerful figure. Was that the problem? Was that why she was so scratchy and bad-tempered? She was with a man who on the surface appeared the perfect companion for a desert-island idyll, to whom she reacted in a way she had long thought impossible. But he wasn't perfect — far from it. She looked up at him. 'Zoe will be concerned about you as well,' she said, hoping to shame him.

'Zoe isn't expecting me.'

'No?' Had he made some excuse to drop her at the dock and run now he'd got his money? Was there someone else waiting for him? 'Someone will surely be worrying?'

'A girl on every island?' he offered, as if he could read her mind and she blushed a deeper pink than the heat from the fire could quite account for.

'Except this one,' she snapped back.

'Except this one,' he agreed, unconcerned by her hostility. 'I prefer my women warm-hearted and generous.'

'With long, shiny hair.'

'Nice,' he agreed, 'but not essential.' But the warm heart and generosity were? she thought. Particularly the generosity. 'Here, I've brought you a hat.' He removed an elderly panama from his head and placed it on hers pulling it down over her eyes. 'Now shall we try that fishing lesson?'

'No, thanks,' she said with a bright smile. 'I'll look after the fire. It wouldn't do to let it out.'

'We'll fish here. You can keep an eye on your fire.' He picked up a rod he had brought from the plane, took her hand

and she was on her feet before she could object.

'But I've never even held a fishing rod,' she objected.

'It's not difficult. I'll show you how.' He led her out into the inlet until the water was lapping around their thighs. Then he made a cast, sending the line flying out towards a tumble of rocks. 'There's a small cave under the water just there where the fish hide.'

'How do you know?'

He turned and looked down at her. 'Trust me. Now take the rod.' He placed it in her hands, standing behind her, holding her shoulders. 'Wind it just a little so the spinner tempts the fish,' he instructed her. 'Like this.' He reached around her and, placing his hands over hers began to reel in the line, very gently.

Maddy laughed and turned to look up at him. 'Could I really catch something?'

'I think it's entirely possible that you already have, Maddy Rufus,' he said, rather brusquely, then the line jerked, would have pulled the rod from her hands if Griff had not been holding it too, and for a few breathless seconds the pair of them wrestled with whatever was on the end of the line, until, without warning, the line went slack and they staggered back together.

'It got away,' she said, laughing a little, breathless too. 'Can we try again?' But this time when she turned to look up at him he stepped back.

'Later.'

'But — '

'Isn't that a boat?'

She turned to scour the horizon and, sure enough, a small, brightly painted dinghy with an outboard engine was moving quite swiftly past the inlet, a little way beyond the reef.

'Well, don't just stand there,' she erupted. 'Do something!'

She raced up the beach to the fire and began fanning it furiously and the flames crackled into life. She threw on a few sappy leaves to produce more smoke then looked up to where Griff was standing near the waters edge. 'Well?' she demanded. 'Did he notice us?'

'He waved back,' Griff said.

'What do you mean, waved back?'

'You said to do something,' he said carelessly, 'so I waved. He waved back.'

'Then he's seen us,' she said with relief. 'Where is he?' She strained to look, but the boat had disappeared.

'He didn't stop.'

'What?' She took a step nearer the edge of the water. 'What do you mean, he didn't stop?'

'I imagine he thought we were camping.'

'Why didn't you shout?' She glared at him furiously, her breast heaving with indignation. 'Damn you, Griff! Why didn't you do something? You just stood there and . . . and . . . waved as if this was a Sunday afternoon picnic.'

'Maddy — ' he began, but she wasn't interested in his excuses. She swung wildly at his chest, pounding at him with her fists, tears of frustration glistening in her eyes.

'I don't believe you want to be rescued.' He caught her wrists but she struggled to free herself, determined to continue her battering. 'This is some big game to you, isn't it? A bit of a joke. Make Maddy Rufus suffer because she was nasty to poor Rupert — '

'Stop it,' he said, and gave her a little shake.

'Well, let me tell you about Rupert — '

He clasped his hand over her mouth. 'I don't want to hear about Rupert, or the rest of your unfortunate lovers . . . '

Driven to impotent fury, she began to kick out at him. Her bare toes made little impression on his shins, but with an exclamation of irritation he shifted his grip on her wrist in order to hold her away from him, and immediately her fist flew upwards, her knuckles catching his lip a sharp, glancing blow.

'Well, big man?' she demanded as he released her mouth with an oath. 'Are you going to hit me back?' Then she gave a little gasp as she realised that she had made a serious mistake.

Maddy wanted to tell him — tell him that she hadn't meant it. Her lips parted to plead with him, but no words came forth; her toffee-coloured eyes only widened like those of a startled gazelle. She wanted to run, escape the ominous darkening of his eyes. But she couldn't. Even if there had been somewhere to run to, she was held fast, riveted, not just by the hand that still grasped her wrist but by the retribution that blazed from Griff's eyes — retribution which, she understood, the slightest movement would bring down upon her head.

For a full second nothing happened, and, letting out the breath she was holding, very slowly, very quietly, she thought she might — just — get away with it. Then as she began to relax he caught her waist and hauled her up into his arms and his mouth came down hard upon hers.

5

Maddy couldn't resist, couldn't fight. Her feet were inches from the ground and she knew with a deep, instinctive knowing that to struggle against his fast hold, his implacable thighs, the hard and dangerous plane of his hips would be utter madness. For a moment she remained determinedly still in his arms while his mouth ground down on her lips, his insistent tongue storming the negligent portcullis of her teeth to take total possession of her mouth.

Her mind tried desperately to shut him out, but the firm stroke of his tongue seemed, in a moment, to steal away her will, sapping her resistance to his determined, blissful assault upon her senses as he explored the secret, sensitive places of her mouth with the skill of a master. A warmth was gradually stealing through her body, making her conscious as never before of the yearning tension of her breasts as they peaked against the smooth cloth of her swimsuit, longing for the rougher touch of the hair that darkened the glistening, sun-drenched skin of his chest. A trembling heat surged through her abdomen, flooded her thighs with a delicious ache that urged her to press closer to him as her body rejected the intellectual games her mind was playing.

It had recognised the sexual tension that had ignited between them the second their eyes had met and now her arms wound themselves about his neck and her body invited him in. For a long, blissful moment she felt the warm, muscle-packed flesh of his shoulders quiver beneath the spread of her fingers, his hair-roughened thighs against her own, smooth skin, the more urgent thrust of his desire as he held her close. Then, as suddenly as it had begun, it was over. With an almost painful rejection, he thrust her away from him, his hands still hard about her waist as she swayed uncertainly, her legs turned to butter that was melting under the heat of his kiss.

For a moment they stood locked together in shocked silence, while Maddy's heart thumped painfully beneath her ribs. Griff's expression was adamantine, impenetrable. 'It would have been a great deal more sensible if I had done what I'd first intended,' he said, a little breathlessly.

'What were you going to do to me, Griff?' Maddy's breath caught in her throat as she tilted her head to look up at him in an unconsciously seductive gesture, her heavy lids reducing her eyes to golden, glittering almonds, her mouth darkly full, throbbing from his cavalier treatment.

He released her waist so rapidly that she would have staggered, perhaps fallen but for her hands about his neck. But he cruelly disengaged them, stepping quickly back to put some distance between them. 'I should have put you over my knee and spanked you the first moment you looked at me like that,' Griff said, his voice like a rasp on wood. 'You are positively dangerous.'

Dangerous? He was blaming her for what happened? Maddy snapped instantly out of the languid state that had pervaded her limbs so thoroughly that she'd hardly known what she was doing or saying. 'Dangerous?' she demanded on a sharp, angry breath. 'Lay one finger on me again, 'Griff will do',' she flared up at him, 'and I promise you'll find out just how dangerous I am.' Her voice caught painfully in her throat, but she didn't stop. 'I'll see you in court.'

For one long, terrible moment his dark eyes regarded her with contempt, then he looked pointedly around. 'Why don't you call a policeman?' he said. With that he turned and walked swiftly away, as if he couldn't bear to be near her, clambering over the rocks at the far end of the beach and disappearing from sight.

Maddy groaned and dropped to the sand as her legs refused to support her any longer; she laid her forehead upon her knees and rocked from side to side. He couldn't have made his point clearer. They were alone, she had encouraged him quite shockingly and but for his restraint they would even now be lying on the foreshore locked in . . . It was awful — the most truly awful thing that had ever happened to her. The man had kissed her not from desire; if he had wanted to make love to her that might have excused her wanton response. But he despised her, had been punishing her.

Not that he was entirely immune, but then it would have taken a block of wood not to respond to the way she had thrown herself at him, and his arousal had been palpable. Yet he had still walked away. Gone fishing. And his invitation to join him had clearly been withdrawn. Nevertheless, she was going to have to bite the bullet, face his contempt and apologise for that stupid remark about taking him to court. It was clearly her week for eating humble pie.

'Oh, Zoe!' she murmured painfully. 'Why on earth did you get involved . . . ?'

She stifled a moan and, tearing off her T-shirt, she threw it to one side and flung herself into the sea. She would have liked to have stripped away the swimsuit too and let the cool, sharp sea-water scrub her naked body clean as she swam the length of the lagoon and back in a fierce overarm. But she didn't dare. She had already exposed far too much. Griff had known she desired him even before she'd known it herself, had accused her of flirting with him. Even now, as she powered through the water trying to rid herself of the taste of him, the scent of his skin, the feel of his hands on her body, she didn't understand why she did desire him. She had been hurt — desperately hurt — by a man who'd wanted nothing but her money. Maybe she was flawed in some way, drawn to that cruel streak . . .

As she tired, she rolled onto her back and floated, drifting where the water would take her, staring up at a totally blue sky. Maybe it was simpler than that, more basic. Perhaps her young body longed for fulfilment and had recognised and reached out to the attractions of Griff's untamed, almost barbaric masculinity. And, trapped in paradise, she had no escape from her feelings.

Maddy finally staggered back up the beach, collapsed in a heap by the dying remains of her fire and poked at it in a desultory fashion. She'd seen nothing to excite her interest other than a yacht on the horizon, too far away to notice them, and the only aircraft that had passed overhead had been high-flying intercontinental jets. Paradise Island seemed to be just off the well-beaten inter-island air and sea lanes.

She sighed, retrieved the panama from the sand where it had fallen and fanned herself with it. It was hot and it would be getting hotter. It was probably better to relax and wait for rescue like Griff. No doubt by tomorrow Zoe would have worked up enough steam for both of them and got everyone running around in circles as she organised a search for her missing goddaughter. Griff's last radio contact had been at the approach to Paradise Island so the search would certainly begin there. She would just have to be patient. And very polite.

She shifted as the heat dried and tightened her skin. Despite her fiery colouring Maddy had been blessed with the delicate olive skin of her French mother, but that still didn't mean that she could sit all day in the fierce tropical sun. She gathered up her T-shirt and slipped it over her shoulders and applied more sunblock to her legs and arms and neck. Then she didn't know what to do with herself.

She was feeling confused and angry and very stupid — emotions totally alien to her forthright nature. Wrapping her arms about her knees and propping her chin on her hands, Maddy looked uncertainly in the direction that Griff had taken.

She ought to go after him, tell him that she didn't mean what she had said in the heat of the moment. It would be difficult to face him, but she knew it was always a mistake to let misunderstandings fester.

Maddy jammed her hat back on her damp, unruly hair and hid her eyes behind dark glasses, telling herself that it was the sun she was protecting herself from, not Griff's scornful eyes. Nevertheless, she rose with extreme reluctance to her feet and began to follow the footprints he had impressed upon the sand.

Scrambling over the rocks at the far end of the beach, she found herself in another, much smaller cove, but it was as deserted as the one she had left, with only a few tell-tale footprints leading to the water's edge.

Her heartbeat raised a fraction. She had been so certain that Griff would be propped lazily against a rock with a fishing line trailing out into the water that the total emptiness of the beach came as a shock

'Griff?' she called uncertainly, and was horrified by the little waver of doubt that had crept into her voice. Impatient with herself, she lifted her hand to shade her eyes, slowly sweeping the surface of the bay in expectation that he had taken to the water. But only the gentle ruffling of the breeze disturbed the palest turquoise water near the shore. Further out the colour deepened patchily to jade, celadon, heart of emerald, and for a moment she anxiously searched the shadows, looking for him beneath the water.

Then she snapped her fingers at her own gullibility. He had almost certainly swum into the next bay and was probably at this moment laughing into his beard. And she had come crawling after him intent on apology. Well, he could sit and stew for all she cared; she was perfectly happy with her own company.

She settled in the inviting shade of a

huge rock and dabbled her feet in a pool left by the retreating tide. A small crab scuttled out of sight in a cloud of sand and Maddy leaned forward to examine the pool a little more closely, stirring the sandy bottom with her toe, watching the tiny tell-tale flurries with a thoughtful expression. He could keep his rotten fish, too. She would force him to acknowledge that she wasn't the helpless bimbo he so obviously took her for.

Maddy returned to the aircraft. Her cosmetic bag yielded a small pair of scissors and she sacrificed a pair of black silk stockings to provide herself with a shrimping net. It took a while to fashion a plaited vine into a hoop to keep it open at the neck, but time was the one thing she wasn't short of, she reminded herself as she cut herself a cane and bound the net to it with the leg of her stocking.

'Move over, Tarzan,' she said, with a soft laugh as she whipped the finished net back and forth and discovered to her considerable satisfaction that everything held together. 'This Jane is about to catch her own lunch.'

She wasted no time but with great concentration began to trawl her makeshift net just beneath the surface of the sand and prod about under the rocks, scooping up the transparent, barely visible little shrimps as they scuttled for cover, shaking them carefully from her net into the shell of a coconut. There was something pleasurably atavistic in the process of hunting for her own food, she discovered, focusing on her task with the same earnestness that she would have applied to a new business proposition. It was the way she did everything — all or nothing.

'Enjoying yourself?' So intent was she upon her labours that the unexpected sound of Griff's voice above her made her whole body jump. He was standing behind one of the larger rocks, his arms folded upon it, his chin propped upon his hands, watching her. She had the impression that he had been there for some time. The bronzed skin of his shoulders was already dry, his recent immersion in the sea betrayed only by the tiny drops of water that swooped along the dark, tangled mop of his hair, to fall and trickle in tiny rivulets down his strongly corded neck. For a moment she watched them, mesmerised, then she straightened abruptly, hoping he wouldn't notice the warmth that flooded into her cheeks.

As it happened, he wasn't looking at her at all but regarding her catch with considerable interest. 'Tasty little things,' he observed. 'How are you going to cook them?'

'Cook them?' She had been so intent upon catching her potful of shrimps that she hadn't given a thought to what came next. Her previous experience of shrimps had been of the pink, cooked variety, from the fishmonger. But she wasn't going to admit that. 'I'll think of something,' she said.

'You certainly seem to have a gift for

improvisation,' he agreed genially, reaching out one long arm and taking the net from her unresisting hand to examine it more closely. Then he raised those taunting eyes of his and she had the uncomfortable suspicion that somewhere, deep inside, he was laughing at her. 'Tell me, Miss Madeleine Osborne, do you *really* wear black silk stockings?'

Maddy flushed as deeply as if she had been caught parading in them for his titillation. 'Never on the beach,' she replied stiffly, and snatched the betraying net out of his hand.

He tilted his eyebrows tormentingly. 'What a pity,' he said, but before she could erupt he lifted a couple of bright red fish threaded onto a line for her inspection. 'You won't be wanting one of these, I take it?'

'I'm sure you can manage them both,' she replied, investing her voice with all the chill she could muster. 'Please don't feel you have to wait for me.'

He inclined his head in the direction of her proposed meal. 'Oh, I won't,' he said. 'It'll be nightfall before you've caught enough of those to fill a tooth.'

'I've caught dozens of the things,' she protested.

'All shell and head, though. I'll see you later.' He finally gave in to the temptation to grin. 'Much later.'

'Damn,' she muttered under her breath as he disappeared from sight, but she wasn't absolutely certain why.

The delicious scent, a little while later, of fish grilling over an open fire reminded her that it was a considerable time since breakfast, and she eyed her catch doubtfully. The shrimps wriggling in the dark recesses of the coconut husk looked very much alive . . . and suddenly very unappetising. But she had decided to make a point, prove she didn't have to rely upon a mere male for her food, and she would have to go through with it. Abandoning her net by the pool, unwilling to parade her mutilated stockings for Griff's further amusement, and holding the husk containing her reluctant lunch very carefully, she clambered back over the rocks to the larger beach.

Griff had speared his catch on a long cane which he had propped across two flat rocks placed either side of the hot embers of the fire and he was laid back on the sand, relaxing while they cooked, his hands clasped behind his head, his eyes closed. He accomplished his objectives with such economy of effort, she thought a little enviously, removing her hat and using it as a fan. 'Do you think you've finally caught enough?' he asked without opening his eyes.

'Yes, thank you,' she said, giving him a wide berth as she walked to the far side of the fire and sank to her knees. She regarded the shrimps with foreboding. They were still very much alive and kicking in their temporary home.

Griff rolled up into a sitting position and offered her a sliver of cane. 'I thought you might like to follow my example,' he said, indicating his own lunch. 'They shouldn't take long to cook.'

Maddy looked up, a little surprised that he should bother to take so much trouble after the way she had threatened him. 'Thank you,' she said. The cane was long and sharp and the idea of using it to spear her helpless captives made her feel suddenly quite sick.

'My pleasure, Miss Osborne.' The brackets at the corners of his mouth deepened slightly. It wasn't quite a smile — she didn't know precisely what it was — but it disturbed her and she wished he wouldn't do it.

'Whatever happened to Maddy Rufus?' she asked, putting off the moment when she had to tackle the lunch.

'It no longer annoys you,' he said tormentingly. Besides, since I've been threatened with the law, a little more formality is called for.' It was clear that the threat did not concern him greatly.

'You — ' she flared, then stopped. It was not what Griff had done that had

151

caused the problem but her own unexpectedly wanton response . . . Her pulse began to thump at the still vivid memory of the way he had kissed her, the way she had kissed him back. Stupid conversation. 'I didn't mean it,' she said, quickly looking away from the steady regard of eyes masked behind tinted lenses that filtered out his expression and the colour that seemed to vibrate with his feelings. She knew it was the moment to apologise, but the words seemed to stick in her throat.

Embarrassed by her own shortcomings, Maddy dropped her gaze to the coconut husk and the wriggling shrimps that were destined to be her lunch and suddenly knew that she would never eat another shrimp in her entire life. But, aware of Griff's mocking scrutiny, she felt unable to back down and admit defeat. With a small gulp, she caught one of the creatures between her fingers and held it to the point of the cane. It was all legs and waving feelers and Maddy could see its tiny organs pulsating through its transparent body. A convulsive shiver ran through her body and suddenly Griff's hand was clasped about her wrist, steadying the tell-tale shake.

'Do you require assistance, Miss Osborne?'

'No!' She dropped the cane. 'I just think I'd prefer a banana for my lunch.'

She had expected him to gloat but he didn't. 'No need for that, Maddy Rufus. The snapper's just about done,' he said, taking the shrimp from her trembling fingers and dropping it back into the husk with its companions and finally meeting her eyes. 'But you're beginning to get the hang of things. I'll certainly give you ten for effort. Nil for execution.'

'I don't want anything from you.'

'No?'

'No! But what about . . . ?' She looked guiltily at her catch; it seemed even worse to deprive them of life and then not eat them out of squeamishness.

'Come on,' he said, taking her elbow and drawing her to her feet, his touch mercifully brief as he bent to pick up the shrimps and hand them to her. 'You can put them back in the pool.'

'Do you think they'll survive?' she asked, suddenly as anxious as if they were a tankful of pet goldfish.

'They've a better chance there than on a skewer,' he pointed out somewhat wryly, and she shuddered, lifting one hand to cover her mouth at the thought, swallowing hard.

'I'm afraid I lack the killer instinct,' Maddy said as she released her lunch to live another day, watching thankfully as the shrimps immediately buried themselves in a flurry of sand that clouded the water.

'Oh, don't underrate yourself,' Griff said. 'Like most women, I'm sure you're more at home in the drawing room, stalking larger game.'

In the sheer relief of returning her captives to the freedom of the water, Maddy had momentarily forgotten his hostility. Now she turned on him, determined once and for all to clear up any misunderstanding, but, confronted with the expressionless stare of his dark glasses, the hard line of his mouth, she suddenly felt it safer to leave things as they were. Hostile.

'I'm sorry to disappoint you, Griff, but I don't have much time to waste swanning about drawing rooms.' Maddy pushed past him, gritting her teeth as her shoulder brushed against his arm and sent a dangerous flutter of desire shivering down her spine, her body determined on a perilous course of its own.

'I'd better go and get some fresh water,' she said as they returned in silence to the fire, anxious to put some distance between them and get a grip on herself.

'It's done.' And he scooped out a half-shell of fresh, clean water and handed it to her. She hesitated, unwilling to take it and risk the dangerous touch of his fingers. 'I thought you wanted this,' he prompted, and she was certain he knew, understood her fear. She took the shell quickly, spilling a little, drinking it quickly so that she could retreat to a safer distance, but he continued, impersonally enough, 'I thought you were going to man your signal fire day and night until you were rescued,' he said, sinking back onto the sand. 'Why did you abandon it?'

'Simple logistics,' she said, happy enough to change the subject.

He raised a brow. 'Are logistics ever simple?'

'In this case, indisputable. Not a single aircraft has passed overhead since we've been here, apart from high-flying jets. But then you undoubtedly already knew that we are off the inter-island air routes. And if the local fishermen simply think we're having a barbecue there isn't a great deal of point in trying to attract their attention that way.'

He shrugged. 'They're used to seeing me here.'

'Are they?' She frowned. 'Why?'

'I like it here.' She waited, but he didn't elaborate.

'In that case, why did you ask me to build a fire in the first place?'

'It seemed a good idea to keep you occupied,' he admitted. 'Despite that rather — ' he paused to consider his words ' — *spirited* manner, I was afraid you might fall apart at the seams when you realised the island was deserted. Mercifully you didn't.'

'If that was meant to be a compliment, Griff, I have to tell you that your technique leaves something to be desired. Perhaps you should consider taking lessons.'

'You wouldn't want me to say something I didn't mean, would you?' His voice trailed a challenge.

'There doesn't seem to be any danger of that,' she snapped back.

'None whatever,' he affirmed, leaning forward to take the fish from the fire, carefully transferring them to the waiting banana-leaf plates. Then he looked at her. 'I never say anything I don't mean, Maddy. Remember that.'

'Very commendable,' she said quickly

157

as his direct gaze brought a fierce blush to her cheeks. 'What a pity your honesty doesn't extend in other directions.' He glanced up, tilting his brow at a questioning angle, and Maddy wondered just how many hearts he had broken with that one look. Was Zoe merely the latest in a long line? 'You're obviously in the habit of taking advantage of the owner's frequent absences to use this island as if it were your own,' she said.

'Am I?' The lines at the corners of his mouth deepened suspiciously. 'Well, I'm sure he doesn't miss a few coconuts, or the odd pineapple.'

His amusement was even more infuriating than his rudeness and demonstrated his lack of scruples very adequately. 'Whether he misses them or not is hardly the point, they aren't yours to take.'

'You didn't object at breakfast,' he pointed out, with some justification. 'In fact, I would say you didn't give the matter a moment's thought.'

'This is an emergency,' she blustered. 'Altogether different. I'm not sneaking about taking advantage of his unwitting hospitality and I shall make a point of writing and thanking him as soon as we're picked up.'

'Don't expect him to be overwhelmed by your finishing-school manners,' he warned. 'He's not the type.'

'Whilst I hate to disabuse you of one of your prejudices about me,' she said carefully, 'it might interest you to know that I cycled to the local comprehensive school every day, come rain or sun, until I was eighteen years old and my 'finishing' consisted of a course in Business Studies at the nearest technical college.' She had refused to move away from her friends and go to the fancy boarding-school her father had favoured when he'd finally reached the point at which he stopped chasing banks and they started chasing him. 'And I'm fluent in French not because of some expensive tuition but because my mother came from France and had

159

an aversion to everything English, particularly the language.' Griff was regarding her with a puzzled, questioning look. 'Don't you believe me?' she demanded.

He shrugged, carelessly. 'Why shouldn't I? If you say your mother is French — '

'Was. I said she *was* French. I no longer have a mother; her aversion to everything English included my father. But I didn't mean that — I meant about my schooling, my life.'

He lifted heavy lids to probe her face and suddenly Maddy regretted her outburst about her mother, certain that she had rather foolishly overreacted to his torments. 'It matters to you what I believe?' he asked.

Did it? Oddly she found that it mattered rather more than she would have believed possible. 'I don't tell lies,' she said. Then, because she had said far more than she'd intended, she quite deliberately changed the subject. 'Why don't you tell me about the mysterious owner of Paradise Island?'

'There's nothing mysterious about him. Except . . . ' He paused, a tiny light dancing in his eyes.

'Yes?'

'Except that the locals call him the Dragon Man.'

'The Dragon Man?' Maddy's eyes widened slightly. 'Good lord, does he breathe fire?'

He laughed softly. 'On occasion . . . '

'But . . . who is he really?'

'I'm sorry, Maddy; you'll have to ask Zoe that.'

'He's a friend of Zoe's?'

'He's very fond of her.'

Fond enough to help her godmother out of the mess she seemed to be in? Fond enough to send 'Griff will do' packing? 'What's he like?'

'What do you want to know, Maddy Rufus?'

'Everything you can tell me. You can't be too careful and I wouldn't want Zoe getting mixed up with the wrong type of man . . . ' Her hint made no impression on him.

'Oh, I'm sure *you'd* approve. Gossip says that he's loaded.'

'Well, that's a good start,' she said brightly.

'I understand that it's the start and the end as far as you are concerned,' he said.

'Understand? More gossip?' He gave her a sharp glance and she had the oddest impression that she had caught him on a raw spot. 'It's really so wide of the mark that I'm tempted to ask you to repeat it,' she continued, enjoying for once the feeling of having gained the upper hand. 'I enjoy a good joke. But I realise it would be miles beneath you to repeat unsubstantiated tittle-tattle.'

'Unsubstantiated?'

'Obviously. I'm not looking for a husband, and even if I were money wouldn't be a consideration — '

'Then it's not true that your father is thinking of setting up a charitable trust with the majority of his fortune? Won't that leave you a little short?' Maddy's brows drew down sharply at this. The trust was far beyond the thinking stage and for her own reasons she had encouraged and supported her father every step of the way, but it was still highly confidential — certainly not the subject for poolside gossip. Had her father told Zoe? 'Before you answer,' Griff continued unwaveringly, 'I refer you to the statement you made earlier about never telling lies.'

'No comment,' she snapped. 'And, to return to the subject of this conversation, I was thinking about Zoe, not myself. I wouldn't want her to get hurt by some ruthless fortune-hunter. How long have you known her, Griff?' For a moment her amber eyes challenged him, but he merely frowned a little, his eyes all question, and, suddenly flustered, she indicated the fish. 'Are we going to eat these, or study them as works of art?'

6

Griff gave her an old-fashioned look as he handed her one of the snappers. 'They should be cool enough to handle,' he remarked.

She tried a piece. 'It's delicious,' she said quickly.

'I hope you still feel the same way in a week,' he replied, a little wryly.

'A week!' Her voice rose to an uncharacteristic squeak and Griff's eyes gleamed wickedly. 'Oh, very funny!'

'I'm glad it amused you. I wonder if you'll still find it funny seven days from now?'

'I'll swim for it long before then,' she declared fervently, then added quickly, 'Tell me some more about the Dragon Man. And I'd already worked out for myself that anyone who can afford to keep a Caribbean island all to himself must have more money than he knows what to do with.' A sudden thought struck her. 'It was his yacht Zoe was on the other night, wasn't it?'

'That's very quick of you.'

'The name is something of a give-away,' she said, thinking hard. Griff, it seemed, had competition. 'He must have tons of money,' she said with considerable satisfaction. 'Did he inherit it, or did he earn it by the sweat of his brow?'

'Does it matter how he came by his money?'

'It would to me. But then, I'm picky.'

'So I noticed.' He shrugged as if he'd expected nothing better. 'I'm sorry to disappoint you, Maddy, but the owner of this island is not one of your pretty aristocrats with a family fortune to play with. Ten years ago he had nothing but enthusiasm and an idea. He's your original fourteen-hour-day, sweat-of-the-brow man.'

'He actually earned enough to buy this island?' she asked, astonished. 'That fabulous yacht?'

'I believe he even has a little to spare for the necessities of life,' he replied.

'Honestly?' Maddy demanded, suddenly suspicious.

He laid his hand upon his heart. 'Scout's honour.'

'I didn't doubt what you said, Griff. I meant . . . ' His eyes sparked dangerously and she gave an awkward little shrug. 'Well, you know what I meant.'

'Yes, I know what you meant,' he said almost angrily. 'But he's not a crook.' As if aware that he had overreacted, he turned away and looked towards the plane pulled up on the shoreline, swinging a little on the high tide. 'Actually, he started the Inter-Island Transport Group ten years ago with that aircraft.'

She followed his glance towards the single-engined seaplane lifting gently on the high tide and stared at the fierce little red dragon on its tail — a dragon now borne by a large fleet of modern aircraft and ferry boats that plied the islands.

166

'So that's why he's called the Dragon Man,' she said. 'And he sold his first plane to you?' She was astonished. 'How on earth could he bear to part with it? If it had been mine I would have parked it outside my office and polished it once a week just for luck.'

'Would you?' For a moment his face softened. 'Well, as you can see, I take good care of it for him.'

'On the outside,' she agreed. It was quite beautiful in fact. 'But if you're planning to follow his example and build a transport empire you'll need to give a little attention to maintenance,' she said, half joking, then turned and stared at him. Was that how he had managed to extract so much money from Zoe? Had he spun her some tale about wanting to start a business of his own? What secrets did his eyes conceal in their ocean depths? She turned quickly away before she drowned and never found the answers. 'I suppose it takes that kind of ruthlessness to build an empire,' she said quickly, and laughed to cover the shake in her voice. 'I'll have to try a little harder not to be sentimental . . . '

'I would never have put you down as sentimental, Maddy. Except of course, about shrimps . . . ' he teased, his eyes creasing at the corners.

Maddy swallowed. 'Oh, I'm hopeless,' she rattled on. 'I still have a dreadful old machine I learned to type on. It's practically a museum piece, but I wouldn't part with it for the world.'

'And you do a lot of typing?' He took one of her hands and examined it. 'I don't think so. Not with those nails.' For a moment her fingers lay in his and she stared at them, briefly held by the contrast of the pale, polished ovals of her nails against his hand.

Abruptly she pulled away. 'Not a lot,' she declared. 'My secretary takes most of the strain these days.'

'You have a secretary?' This seemed to surprise him. 'Zoe said you have some little agency — a hobby to keep you busy. I didn't get the impression it rated a secretary. But then I suppose you wouldn't want to be tied down to an office; it would seriously cut down the time you could spend on tropical beaches.'

'A month isn't much out of three years — ' she began, then stopped. She had no reason to justify herself to this man. 'It sounds as if you and Zoe spent a considerable amount of time discussing me,' she said with just a hint of exasperation.

He didn't flinch from her accusing eyes. 'Perhaps she did run on a little . . . she was somewhat upset the other night.' 'Upset'? Zoe had spoken her mind, but 'upset' overstated the case a little. 'And I'm a good listener.'

Part of the stock-in-trade of a conman, no doubt, she thought caustically. 'Zoe made her feelings perfectly clear at the time. There was no need for her to discuss it with you.'

'I think it was your reaction to her talk with you that so upset her.'

'But I thought she understood . . . '

Then she sighed. Maybe not. She loved Zoe, but her godmother had a very personal way of looking at things, which made her just a little exasperating at times. 'I swear if I told her that I was planning to open a branch in Paris she would just assume it was to make it simpler to get to the spring and autumn collections,' she muttered, half to herself.

'And are you? Planning to open a branch in Paris?' His hearing was clearly acute, his insolent amusement wounding. Maddy had worked hard for her success and didn't like being mocked. But she wasn't about to let it show.

She laid the tips of her fingers against her breast. '*Moi?*' she said, opening her eyes very wide, apparently incredulous that he could possibly have taken her seriously.

Griff's eyes narrowed as he regarded her with a thoughtful expression and Maddy had the uncomfortable feeling that she had gone just a little too far.

Heaven alone knew what nonsense her godmother had filled Griff's head with, and he'd seen enough to colour his own opinion a very nasty shade of disapproval; now she seemed hell-bent on making it worse. Why couldn't she just have said yes, for heaven's sake? *It's none of your business. Mr 'Griff will do', but my 'little hobby' is so successful that I've decided to expand into Europe.*

What on earth was it about the man that made her react like that? *Maybe because he's the first man you've come across that you can't control, can't run away from, and it frightens you to death,* her subconscious prompted helpfully.

Maddy felt her sun-warmed cheeks flush a shade darker. Rubbish, she thought, consigning her subconscious to the dustbin. Absolute rubbish. This conversation had nothing to do with her. It was Zoe who mattered.

'What is it?'

Maddy's glance collided with the

clear, penetrating stare of her fellow castaway. 'Nothing,' she said, with an unconvincing little laugh as she quickly attempted to turn the conversation and her thoughts to less dangerous channels. 'I've just realised why no planes fly over the island, that's all.'

'Oh?' His voice was soft as thistle-down, yet insistent, not to be ignored.

'Your Dragon Man has obviously arranged it that way,' she said, making a brave attempt to ignore the ripple of goose-flesh on her skin. 'I don't suppose he wants to be reminded of work when he's on a back-to-nature kick.'

'You could be right,' Griff agreed, his eyes still holding hers.

'And I'm glad he's got his island,' she continued a little desperately. 'Even if he doesn't have much time to visit it. Anyone who has earned his money the *hard* way knows how to appreciate what he's got.'

'He appreciates it,' he said intently. Then, as he turned to stare out to sea, his eyes finally released her.

Relief mingled with an almost palpable sense of loss and she wrapped her arms about her legs and laid her chin on her knees. 'Not too often, I hope, for your sake. I can quite see that it wouldn't suit you to have the owner in residence,' Maddy said, then added a wicked little afterthought. 'Of course, if he marries Zoe he might build a home here. She was very taken with the villa on Mustique. That would put your fishing trips on permanent hold.' He began to choke and Maddy leapt to her feet and scrambled behind him, clasping him under the ribs, but before she could do more he grabbed her hands and stopped her.

'No,' he said, a little huskily, looking over his shoulder, his face so close to hers that she could almost feel the faint stubble that darkened his jaw. For a second neither of them moved, his hands upon hers locking them together, her arms about him holding her body close to the warmth of his back, her cheek touching the pulse of his strongly corded neck, her lips within reach of the chiselled line of his jaw. Her mouth parted slightly and she moistened it with the tip of her tongue. Abruptly he released her. 'I'm fine,' he said curtly.

Maddy sat back on her heels, her face scarlet. 'I'm sorry. I thought you were choking on a fishbone . . . ' she mumbled, covering her embarrassment by scooping him some water from the bucket, but unable to meet his eyes as she passed it to him. 'I did this first-aid course . . . '

'You must have passed with flying colours if the speed of your reaction is anything to go by,' he said; his voice was gentler than she'd expected. 'But I think it was just shock.'

'Shock?' Her brows drew together in a little frown and he gave an odd little shrug. 'Do you mean at the idea of building a vast villa on Paradise Island?'

'There's no danger of that,' he said.

'Oh.'

'You sound disappointed.'

'I'd like Zoe to find someone who will make her happy ... someone kind ...'

'I don't think she'd be happy on an uninhabited island for very long.'

'With the right man, who'd be unhappy?'

He reached out and touched her lips warningly with the tip of one finger. 'Have a care, Maddy; you're beginning to sound almost human ...'

Maddy pulled back, jolted by that touch. 'Nonsense. I wasn't talking about me.' His eyes refused to believe her. 'Of course, you're right about the villa,' she said briskly, not wanting to probe the reasons for such unlooked for wistfulness. 'Paradise Island needs something less theatrical, something to blend into the surroundings so that, flying over the island, you would never know anyone had ever set foot upon it.' He smiled and shook his head, clearly amused. 'What?' she demanded.

'Nothing, nothing ... Tell me, Maddy, what would you build here, if the island belonged to you?'

'Me?' Relieved to be on safer ground, she rolled over onto her stomach and propped her chin on her hands, staring up at the island rising steeply away from the beach, thinking how wonderful it would be to come here to your own hide-away whenever you wanted to. But lonely too. She glanced at Griff; then away again quickly. He couldn't be the right man. He was a conman, a thief of hearts. But not hers. Hers was safely under lock and key. Then why isn't the burglar alarm ringing?

'Well?' She jumped as he interrupted the taunt of her subconscious and gratefully she gave her undivided attention to this much safer topic.

'Well,' she said quickly, 'I think I'd want to use thatch or wooden shingles for the roof — '

'What about rot?' he interrupted. 'It can be very humid at certain times of the year.'

'I didn't realise this exercise had

anything to do with reality,' she objected.

'And if it had?'

'I . . . well . . . ' For a moment she almost believed he meant . . . No! This was all pure fantasy. A game. 'If you're going to worry about such mundane details, I'm sure it wouldn't be a problem with modern preservatives,' she said, airily dismissing his concern.

'All right,' he said, laughing, and the sound pleased her; it was rich and warm — something he should do more often. Maddy waved a hand to take in the curve of the beach.

'It should be set back from the beach, a little way up the hill to take advantage of the shade.' And she began to see it in her mind. 'Hardly what you could call a house — more a series of rooms, very open to catch the sea breezes, the water could easily be piped down . . . Solar power . . . ' She caught herself as she saw him smile and she realised that her enthusiasm was running away with her — a fault her accountant was always trying to curb. But then what was life without enthusiasm?

'And when it rains?'

'What a pessimist you are,' she chided. 'I'd have wide verandas.'

'Wide verandas? I'd never have thought of that,' he teased. 'How wide?'

It was a game, she reminded herself, and buried the feeling that there was something else happening beneath the surface.

She took a deep breath. 'Absolutely vast,' she declared fervently. 'Shaped to carry away the rainwater to a small pool where I'd keep pet shrimps that must never, ever be eaten, on pain of life banishment.'

'Even if you were starving?'

'On Paradise Island? With its endless supply of fish and coconuts and bananas and who knows what else if you were to look?' She raised her hand solemnly. 'I hereby declare I shall never eat another shrimp in my entire life.'

Griff lifted his hand and placed his

palm against hers, matching her fingers against his own. 'I can live with that.' For a moment neither of them moved, while the air shimmered with something unspoken, undreamed of, and Maddy's insides seemed to roll over like a puppy inviting play. Griff abruptly dropped his hand. 'You obviously have a talent for this sort of thing,' he said. 'Rather more sympathy with your surroundings than Zoe.'

Mention of her godmother brought Maddy crashing back to the present and her immediate predicament. 'I wonder if she's phoned Dad and told him what's happened?' she mused anxiously. 'He'll be worried to death.'

Griff looked away. 'She won't worry him unnecessarily. How was the fish?' he asked, changing the subject.

She looked at the heap of bones on the banana leaf. 'It was quite delicious.' She hesitated. 'Thank you for saving me from the shrimps.'

'I was thinking of myself,' he said briskly, as if regretting that moment when they had come close to something unimaginable. 'You looked as if you were about to be sick.'

'Oh.' Well, that was that.

'Would you like some coconut milk?' he offered politely.

'Only if it means you have to climb a palm tree to pick a nut.'

His mouth twisted into a lopsided grin that did something crazy to her insides. 'I'm afraid not.'

'In that case water will do just fine.' She picked up a coconut husk, but he overturned the bucket before she could dip it in.

'Warm. Very nasty. It's better straight from the stream.' He stood up and held out his hand. Maddy hesitated, remembering their earlier encounter at the waterfall certain that it would be foolhardy to venture there again in his company. There was something drawing her to him — a recognition that she had at last met a man strong enough to take her, if he chose. And, despite his attempts to cover his feelings, resist them, Griff felt it too, she was sure.

'I'm not that thirsty,' she said abruptly. 'Besides, someone might come by.'

'No one is going to come by, Maddy, and it's time to get out of the sun for a while.' He didn't sound as if he was about to take no for an answer. 'I'm sure Jack would be pleased to see you.'

'Well, that will make a nice change,' she said crisply, and was rewarded with the ironical lift of a dark brow. Nevertheless the lure of the cool green forest was very enticing, but she ignored his hand, rising slowly, brushing the sand from her legs. Then she bent to pick up the bucket.

'Leave that.'

'But water-carrying is women's work, remember?'

He grinned broadly, revealing strong white teeth. 'You can fetch some later,' he promised, and Maddy only just managed to bite back the angry retort that flew to her lips. Griff always seemed to be able to top her, no matter what she said. It was time she put her mind to the problem, because no one treated her the way that he did and got away with it. Not for ever.

'How do you know he's called Jack?' she asked as she followed him up the narrow path. Griff halted suddenly, turning his head to stare over his shoulder at her, and Maddy only just managed to prevent herself from bumping into him. 'The parrot,' she explained a little breathlessly. 'How do you know his name?'

His eyes narrowed momentarily, then he gave the smallest shrug and the deepening clefts in his cheeks betrayed just the hint of a smile. 'He told me, of course. That's the advantage of a talking bird.'

She tapped her forehead with the flat of her palm. 'Now why didn't I think of that?'

'There are clearly some glaring gaps in your education,' he replied with perfect seriousness. For a moment Maddy didn't know whether to hit him or laugh. Her sense of the ridiculous won hands down and, unable to help herself, she giggled. It must have been infectious because Griff's smile deepened until there was no doubt that he too found the idea quite ridiculous.

'You should try and find him a mate,' she suggested. 'It doesn't seem right that he's on his own in paradise.'

'You're an unlikely romantic, Maddy.'

'Am I?' She lifted her shoulders a fraction. Not romantic, not sentimental — just how did he see her? She didn't care, she told herself, but she wasn't entirely convinced. 'Life's full of surprises.'

'Isn't it, though? And in fact you're quite right. The St Vincent parrot is an endangered species. Maybe I should catch him and send him to the breeding programme on St Vincent.'

'You? Wouldn't the Dragon Man object?'

'I . . . ' For a moment she thought he was going to say something. Then he threw his arm about her shoulders, drawing her into his side so that they could squeeze up the path together. 'I'll ask him. Come on, Maddy. I believe it's time you saw a little more of Paradise Island than the beach.'

There was a delicious warmth that had nothing to do with the ambient temperature, Maddy discovered, tucked against his firm body as they walked up the path to the pool. Griff stopped to point out a flurry of tiny hummingbirds drinking nectar from the huge scarlet hibiscus flowers, their plumage copper-green in the filtered sunlight. While she watched, he plucked a stem of creamy orchids and, removing her hat, threaded it through her hair.

'Now you look more like a dusky island maiden,' he said. 'The hair's something of a give-away, though.' He pushed a wayward tendril from her brow and tucked it behind her ear.

'It's the humidity,' Maddy said, not quite in control of her voice. 'I've gone rusty.' Then, to cover her blushing confusion, she quickly went on, 'It's almost as if this was once a garden that's gone to seed,' she said, looking about her. Looking anywhere but at Griff.

He followed her gaze. 'Nature's own. Seeds have been brought by the sea and by birds, or on the feet of travellers, and they've found a niche. Everything fits.'

'Except Jack?'

He glanced down at her. 'He's survived. He's made a place for himself. If the wind or chance brings him a mate, then he and his kind will become a part of the island.'

'Even if they push out something else?'

'That's how it's always been.'

'The strong preying on the weak?' she asked pointedly, pulling away from the dangerously seductive circle of his arm.

His brows closed in a frown. 'Yes, Maddy. Since the dawn of time.'

But not if she could help it. She had to get hold of that cheque somehow and send it back to Zoe. Not now. He'd miss it. But when someone came to take them off the island. She'd find a way. They stopped at the pool to drink from water that splashed over the waterfall into their cupped hands. Then Griff climbed onto the rocks and extended his hand to pull her up after him into the cascade of water. 'Come on.'

For a moment she hesitated. 'I know it's ridiculous, but I feel as if I'm trespassing,' she objected.

'This was once a bare volcanic outcrop, Maddy. Everything on it was a trespasser once.'

'But I haven't found my niche.'

'You will.'

'And if I change something?' There was a hint of challenge in her voice. 'Irrevocably?'

'It's a risk we take by being alive. We change places, places change us.

'Do they?' But she knew the answer. She had already changed. She didn't quite know how or in what way. She just felt different. 'You're quite the philosopher, Griff.'

'No. Just your average man wondering what's over the rainbow.' Griff turned to where a single ray of sunlight angling through the canopy high above them caught and split in the spray and a miniature rainbow arched tantalisingly across the cascade, calling her, inviting her to step beyond it and discover some glorious secret. Then he turned back to stare down at her. 'Come with me, Maddy.'

For a moment they remained, poised between earth and sky. Then Maddy reached up to clasp his hand, gasping as he pulled her up through the spray. It showered her face and throat and soaked her T-shirt so that it clung to her, deliciously cooling, outlining her body as she clutched at him unsteadily before finding her footing.

She propped her panama on an overhanging branch, pushed her sunglasses up into her hair and in a gesture of sheer pleasure tilted her head back so that her face caught the sun and her vivid hair hung in the shaft of sunlight, vying with the rainbow for glory. For just a moment Griff held her there, his arm looped about her waist as they balanced on the edge of the waterfall, their bodies almost, not quite, touching. It was primitive and glorious and she saw from Griff's darkening eyes that it was dangerous too. But then, what was paradise without forbidden fruit?

She was dragged back from the brink of some madness by a piercing wolf-whistle, the flash of orange and yellow banding a pair of brown wings, then Jack settled on the branch above them. She stepped free of the almost drugging pleasure of Griff's touch and looked up, anywhere but at his eyes.

'Hello, Jack,' she said a little breathlessly.

'Hello, Jack,' the bird repeated, and put his head on one side in a conspiratorial little movement that brought a smile to her lips.

'We're exploring; care to show us the sights?' she invited with a careless little gesture as she tried desperately to cover the palpitating confusion of her own thoughts. The bird flew down onto a nearby tree and then hopped away to the right, as if leading the way. 'I do believe he is,' Maddy laughed, making a move to follow him, but Griff caught her arm.

'Not that way, Maddy, the ground falls away rather steeply.'

'But there's a path,' she objected. 'It looks quite well-worn.'

'Appearances can be deceptive. And if you slip and hurt yourself — '

'I won't be much use to you as a drawer of water and hewer of wood? I remember.'

'I'm glad you do,' he said, steering her firmly over the stream via a series of well-placed rocks. 'This way takes us to the top of the island. The view is well worth the effort.'

'Perhaps we should have lit our fire up there,' Maddy said a little scratchily as she glanced back at the beckoning path and caught the faint but unmistakable scent of frangipani blossom.

'No, nothing to spoil the perfection . . . ' His hand upon her arm stopped her. 'But I should warn you that there is a risk involved.'

'A risk?'

'Once you've been to the summit of paradise, you may never want to come down.'

Startled by the intensity of his voice, she turned and looked up into his face. 'You really love this place, don't you, Griff?'

For a moment, the space of a heartbeat, she saw something in his eyes, a feeling of great intensity too fleeting to capture, to interpret. Then, as if he realised that he was in danger of exposing some deep personal feeling, he looked away. 'The fishing's great,' he agreed, with a careless gesture that quite definitely put an end to the subject, but Maddy knew that for him it was a great deal more than just a handy place to catch fish. And she wondered how he felt about someone else owning it, but his face betrayed no secrets as he held back a branch that dipped across the path. 'This way, Miss Osborne,' he invited, sketching a bow with mock formality.

She took a tentative step forward and he extended his hand to her. It was square and darkly tanned, with long, strong fingers that bore the scars of a hard life. It didn't look like the hand of a man who spent his life robbing gullible women of their money when there were worlds to conquer. On the contrary, it looked like the hand of a man you could trust with your life. And she had already done just that, she thought, and shivered a little at the recollection of the way he had landed the seaplane. He had not let her down. She met his eyes and was suddenly quite sure that he would never let her down.

Maddy wondered idly if perhaps she had had rather too much sun; she certainly didn't appear to be behaving quite rationally. But then, this wasn't a very rational situation. The poised, efficient Miss Osborne had been cast away on a desert island with the kind of man most girls dreamed about. Not her of course. She was far too sensible to fall for such foolish dreams twice in one lifetime, wasn't she?

Maddy pushed back a strand of hair that had fallen across her forehead and her hand came into contact with the spray of orchids that Griff had tucked behind her ear ... Oh sensible, Miss Osborne, Maddy's subconscious rose to mock her wickedly. With a tiny catch of her breath, as if she was taking some great, irretrievable step, Maddy consigned her subconscious to the dustbin, reached out and placed her hand in his. It looked so fragile, small and pale against his broad palm. Then he closed his hand over hers and she had the clearest feeling that she would never get it back, that Griff had claimed it as his own.

'Shall we go?'

' 'The woods are lovely, dark and deep ... ' ' she quoted huskily.

' 'But I have promises to keep ... ' '

he continued slowly, then his eyes shaded as if he had remembered something, and an odd little shiver rippled down Maddy's spine. 'What's the matter?' he asked as the tremor transmitted itself to him.

'Nothing.' She snapped her hand back to her side. 'I'm just a little wet from the waterfall, that's all. Shall we try and find the sun?'

He turned without a word and led the way up the path. For a moment Maddy stayed where she was, and knew that she was a fool for wishing her hand was still safely tucked up in his. Definitely too much sun. Jack gave a loud squawk from his perch some way above her and then fluttered from tree to tree, retracing the way they had come. She watched him for a moment and, as if aware of her scrutiny, he settled on a bush the other side of the stream near the path, and put his head on one side. Despite Griff's warning she was certain that the bird wanted her to follow him and she took a step towards him, then another.

'Maddy?' She started guiltily and spun round. 'Where are you going?'

'Nowhere,' she said, too quickly. 'Just daydreaming. Sorry.'

He stood back, indicating the path she should take, and she didn't linger, hurrying through the forest, no longer lulled by the incessant, hypnotic hum of insects, hardly even aware of the more strident calls of the mockingbirds. She was lost somewhere inside her head, where Griff's soft, insistent voice was repeating over and over, 'Places change us.' It was true. She was being changed irretrievably by the island. By him.

Then abruptly she burst through the thickly forested slopes and was on top of the world, surrounded on all sides by an ocean sparkling in the sunlight, the broken necklace of the Grenadines disappearing into the afternoon haze, the peaks of Union tantalisingly close, yet as far out of reach as if they were a thousand miles away.

The white wake of motor boats

trailed teasingly in the distance and the snowy sails of a dozen yachts dipped under the breeze, one seeming almost close enough to hail. But it was an illusion, she knew. The wind would whip her voice away, and if anyone was looking in her direction and she was seen waving, who would suppose she could desire rescue? They would do just what Griff's passing fisherman had done and wave back.

It seemed impossible to be stranded so close to so many people and Maddy knew that twenty-four hours ago she would have raged at her impotence. Now she settled on a smooth, sun-warmed rock, startling a tiny, basking lizard which disappeared in the flash of green. She leaned back on her hands, closed her eyes and lifted her face to drink in the fresh, cooling scent of the trade winds. Rescue would come when it came. There was no point in raging against anything. Right now she had nothing more important in the world to do than sit here.

Griff settled very quietly beside her on the stone. She could sense the warmth of his body, the sharp, musky, male scent of him. 'You're right, Griff,' she said, acknowledging his presence without opening her eyes. 'It's beautiful up here.'

'Do you still want to summon some gallant to your rescue?' She turned to him to deny it, but he was offering her a conch shell. 'Put it to your lips and blow,' he suggested. 'Someone might hear you.'

She took the shell between her hands. It was heavy, rough on the outside, but the inside shone with a beautiful peachy-pink lustre. She put it to her ear and listened to the sea for a moment. It was lulling, seductive. 'Not yet,' she said, with a sigh so small that she was hardly aware of it. And she put the shell down on the rock beside her. 'There isn't any rush.'

7

'Maddy?' Griff said her name softly — so softly that for a moment she wasn't certain she had really heard his voice. 'Maddy,' he repeated, as if he could not help himself, and under the soft, hypnotic sound of her name she raised her lids and turned to face him. It seemed almost as if he was moving in slow motion as he raised his hands to capture her face and draw her into his body.

She did not resist, could not — the moment was too perfect, too right. Her lips parted slightly over even white teeth as she waited, her face cradled in his hands, his long fingers threaded in her hair — waited for him to kiss her.

This time he did not crush her soft mouth beneath his, nor did he tease her with a taunting butterfly touch of his lips that left her longing pitifully for more. He bent his head to hers slowly — so slowly that she could see the thick dark fringe of lashes normally hidden behind dark glasses, the tiny flecks of blue in the sea-green of his eyes as he paused, his lips a bare inch from hers. Then his heavy lids closed as his mouth touched hers, and a strange longing, entirely new and yet instantly recognisable, sparked through her.

His lips began to move over hers in the most gentle exploration, greeting her lips, her teeth, the tip of her tongue with his own, as if committing the taste of her to his memory. Maddy remained very still, containing her fervent longing to respond to his caress. The kiss was a gift, from Griff to her, and although her heart was almost bursting with the aching need it stirred deep within her some elemental instinct warned her to be patient, to let him take the lead. When he lifted his head a few moments later, with a shudder that betrayed the intensity with which he had held himself in check, she knew she had been right to hold back. The kiss had been heart-rendingly sweet. A promise? Or, as he knew that rescue must come soon, that they must leave the island, was it simply goodbye?

But for a moment Griff said nothing and she was content enough to lean her head against his shoulder, content to enjoy the clear, fresh scent of the sea carried on the breeze, overlaid with the elusive sweetness of frangipani, content to enjoy the rattle of wind through bamboo, and the poinsettia, a vivid splash of red in the lush vegetation that spread below them — reminder that, despite the heat, Christmas was nearly upon them — and Griff beside her, his dark hair tousled by the breeze, the hard edge of his profile shadowed against the sun.

She lifted her face to look up at him and for a blazing second their eyes met and anything might have happened. Then Griff pulled back. 'I'm sorry, Maddy,' he said, 'I shouldn't have done that.'

Maddy put out her hand, cradled his cheek lightly in her hand. 'It's all right, Griff. I promise I'm not about to summon the constabulary.' Her voice was a shy husky murmur from deep in her throat. 'And I'm not about to scream. Promise.'

'Don't!' He groaned and she withdrew her hand. 'I didn't mean to kiss you, Maddy. Not like that . . . God knows, I didn't mean to. It was wrong.' His sweeping glance took in the island spread at their feet before he turned to her, his eyes as dark as obsidian against the brilliance of the sun, his face shadowed, and suddenly she remembered and guilt stabbed through her.

'Because of Zoe . . . '

Startled, he turned to her. 'You've guessed?'

So it was true. 'You were careless, Griff . . . '

'I knew I'd said too much . . . Maddy . . . '

How could she have ever forgotten? Zoe would be shattered to discover that she had made a fool of herself over a fortune-hunter. How much worse it would be if she discovered that her young lover had made a pass at her god-daughter before he'd even banked the proceeds . . .

'How could you do it?' she asked a little despairingly.

He stood up abruptly. 'I can't expect you to understand. You could never begin to understand how much I owe . . . '

He was in debt? Maddy felt a surge of hope. It was as simple as that? She could handle that. She would return Zoe's cheque, deal with Griff's problems. They would be expensive, no doubt, but she would do anything to save Zoe from the bitter disillusionment of knowing that a man had wanted her only for her money. She looked up into his face. Expensive and dangerous, but there was no other way. The tip of her tongue moistened her dry mouth.

'I want you to forget about Zoe, Griff.' He stiffened, but she ploughed on before she entirely lost her nerve.

'You don't need her. Just tell me what you want; I'll do anything — '

'Stop that!' He seized her arm and shook her. 'For a moment — for just a moment — I hoped, dreamed . . . But I should know better than to rely on a shooting star.' He jerked her close, so that his mouth was threatening hers. 'So, tell me, my beautiful little gold-digger, what is it that you do that drives men crazy? What tricks — ?'

'What . . . what are you talking about?' Bewildered by this sudden change in his manner she tried to step back, but his hand tightened about her arm and she didn't make it.

'I'm cut from a different cloth from the men you play your teasing games with. What the Dragon Man wants — '

'Dragon Man?' Confusion was fogging her mind so that she could hardly think. The Dragon Man? What on earth was he talking about? The Dragon Man wasn't here . . .

'I've always thought, Maddy, that one day you would go too far . . . ' And, seizing the hem of her T-shirt, he pulled it over her head in one smooth movement and tossed it aside. Before her stunned brain could react, he'd hooked his thumbs beneath the straps of her swimsuit and jerked them down over her arms, exposing the milky whiteness of breasts that she had never bared to the sun. There was a moment of shocked silence. 'What the Dragon Man wants,' he repeated, in a low, throaty growl that scorched her very soul, 'he takes. And since you're so generously offering . . . '

Maddy's mind cleared in a sudden flash of understanding, but even as she opened her mouth to demand an explanation he jerked her close, crushing her pitilessly against the iron wall of his chest. And this time his lips were without mercy.

For a moment she was too shocked to react. It was far too long a moment before her fists began raining blows against his shoulders and she began kicking out with her useless sandals that made not the slightest impression. He took everything she could throw at him and still his fingers bit into her shoulders and she had to endure that fierce, loveless kiss.

It was as if he was determined to wipe out every trace of his brief, tender embrace at the summit of paradise, overwrite his memory with something far earthier, more primitive than that most loving touch, reducing it from something splendid to man's most basic instinct.

And as the realisation of what he was doing finally penetrated the turmoil of her confused, bewildered brain Maddy stopped fighting. She accepted gladly the chance to eradicate that moment from her memory, welcoming the savage intrusion of his tongue in the knowledge that it would destroy for ever the sweet taste of his lips and offer her some kind of freedom. If he had wanted to make her hate him, he couldn't have chosen a more effective weapon. And, with all of her heart, she wanted to hate him.

When finally, after what might have been a lifetime, he raised his head and she saw that his eyes were hard, blanked of all expression, she lifted her hand and wiped the back of it across her burning mouth in a heartbreakingly vulnerable gesture that brought a soft oath to his lips.

'What have I ever done to you, Griff?' Maddy demanded, breathless but determined, her eyes blazing in her white face, taking on the question in his bottomless green eyes, flinging it back at him, and for a moment it seemed to shake him.

'Don't you know?' His voice was barely more than a breath. 'Have you no idea — ?' He stopped abruptly, releasing her shoulders without warning so that she stumbled and her foot came sharply up against the root of a tree blown down by some tropical storm that had swept the island long ago. She cried out as she put out a hand to save herself, but with a swiftness of movement that seemed to defy gravity he was there, holding her, cursing under his breath at his own stupidity as he steadied her.

But she jerked away from him, from the burning touch of his hands upon her skin, staggering a little as she broke free, holding him at bay when he would have reached out to help — then blushing fiercely as she saw that his eyes were fixed upon her body. 'For pity's sake, cover yourself . . . ' When, transfixed by embarrassment, she made no move to do so, he caught the straps of her swimsuit and pulled it up.

His touch was sufficient to break the spell that held her and she jerked back, holding her costume to her with her arm as a tiny, anguished moan escaped her lips. 'Don't touch me!' she said with desperate urgency, struggling with the straps. 'I don't want you to touch me ever again.' It was impossible for her to risk that longed-for caress.

How had she ever been stupid enough to believe she could forget his kiss, the extraordinary joy of that moment when she had believed he had meant it? She would try, but she knew it would be a lost cause. Nothing he could do to her would ever destroy that shimmering moment in time when she had been ready to believe . . . anything. She would always remember. If she lived to be ninety-two, the honeyed touch of his lips would still be the most bitter-sweet memory.

'Oh, God, Maddy.' He took a step towards her. 'This is a nightmare. I never meant — '

She held out an imperious hand to stop him. She didn't want to know what he meant. Locked in that maelstrom of passion and pain, she had worked out the bare bones of it for herself. Hugo Griffin was the Dragon Man. The clue had been there in his name all the time. Griffins and dragons were all cut from the same dangerous cloth. Did he mean her to know, or had it just slipped out?

How foolish she had been. How gullible. The dinghy that hadn't stopped. The way he had delayed her when she had tried to light the fire to attract a distant yacht . . . the lighter that had conveniently refused to work until it was too late . . .

'Maddy . . . ' He reached out for her. 'It's my nightmare, not yours, Dragon Man,' she flung at him. Griff bit down hard, his lips thinning as he fought to keep inside whatever it was he wanted to say, man enough to know that he could not apologise for what he had done, that there were no words to cover it. But it was precious little comfort. And, hand still outstretched to keep him at a distance, she walked slowly, carefully around him until she was between him and the path that led back through the forest to the beach. 'I'm going back to the beach,' she said. 'Alone.'

He retrieved her T-shirt, took a step towards her. 'I'd better come with you — '

She snatched the shirt, pulled it over her, feeling too naked in her demure swimsuit. 'Don't! Don't call me Maddy,' she said, her voice oddly calm. This wasn't the moment to scream. Her pain was an icy knot deep inside her, contained too tightly for such an easy release. She wasn't sure that she would ever be able to raise her voice above a whisper again. 'Don't speak to me at all, Hugo Griffin.' How hard it was to say his name! 'From now on I don't want you to do anything for me; I don't want you to come near me.' He didn't say anything but remained perfectly still a foot away from her. 'Is that perfectly clear?' she demanded.

'You wanted me to answer you?' he asked, his eyes glittering dangerously in that small, scented clearing high above the Caribbean. 'I understood I wasn't supposed to speak.' She snapped round, took a step towards the path, but his voice followed her. 'There's no way off this island without me,' he warned.

'Someone will come looking for me. Until they do, just stay away from me.' She turned and half stumbled onto the path.

'Will you be taking up shrimping

again, Maddy Rufus?' he asked very softly, tempting her to a truce, and she faltered, glanced back. But she could never return to that state of armed neutrality that had governed their relationship until now. One tender kiss and she had been prepared to lay down her arms and surrender all too willingly. Dignity was all that remained and precious little of that, but if she stretched it thinly it might just save her.

'The shrimps are safe from me,' she said, with only a little shake in her voice. 'I can survive on water for the next twenty-four hours if I have to. Even Zoe should have got the message by then.'

'And if she hasn't?' He took another step towards her as if he sensed her vulnerability. She didn't wait to find out but stepped back onto the path before turning to run as fast as she dared down the steep, narrow track towards the space and safety of the beach. Once she glanced back — she couldn't see or hear him, but she didn't pause until she was brought to a breathless halt in the glade above the waterfall by the barrier of the stream. The stepping stones seemed further apart than she remembered, or maybe they were just more daunting without his strong arm to cling to as she leapt across.

As she stepped out onto the first stone she saw him out of the corner of her eye, his face riven with concern. 'Maddy, wait!'

But she couldn't wait, mustn't wait. He remained where he was, afraid, perhaps, that any sudden move on his part would initiate disaster, and Maddy locked him out of her head, making the return journey with enormous concentration, determined that she should not slip on the wet stones, give him any excuse to come after her, touch her. Finally she stepped onto the opposite bank with a long sigh of relief and it took all her will-power not to look back.

Jack had disappeared from his perch above the falls, although she fancied she heard his squawk tempting her from somewhere below, down the forbidden path. Maddy did not even look; it held no attraction for her now. She just wanted to get back to the beach. She would be safer there in the bright sunlight, but first she had to negotiate the waterfall. From below, with Griff to pull her up, it had seemed simple enough, but, from above, the ground seemed far away, with the slippery rocks lying in wait to tear at her if she should make the slightest error.

The rattle of a stone warned her that Griff was close behind. 'There's only one way down,' he said, and before she could even register his presence at her side his arm was about her waist, pinning her tight against him. Startled, she glanced up, and he stared down into her face. 'Ready?' He didn't wait for her answer but leapt with her down through the cascading falls and into the dark water of the pool. It was much deeper than she had supposed and they sank, it seemed to Maddy, for ever, his arms and legs wrapped protectively around her, her hair streaming out above them.

For a moment they hung motionless in the water. Griff's face was pale underwater, with dark shadows that made him seem both strange and beautiful, and Maddy thought her heart must break in two. Then he gave a fierce kick with his feet and they were speeding upwards, the water fizzing around them as they erupted, gasping, locked together, the water streaming down their faces. 'Shall we go back and do that again?' he invited, his eyes dark with some unfathomable mystery. And Maddy would have given anything in the world to be able to say yes.

Then she saw the spray of creamy orchids floating on the surface of the water — the flowers that he had picked and threaded through her hair — and a small cry escaped her lips before she clamped them shut on her pain.

She closed her eyes tightly. How could there be pain? She had known the Dragon Man for such a little time. For turbulent, difficult hours, it was true, but he had never hidden the way he felt about her. From the very first moment he had been consistent. Until he had kissed her and melted her heart.

Maddy put her hands against his chest and pushed, turning away from the heady challenge in his eyes, and swam swiftly to the side, where she hauled herself out of the pool. She had lost her sandals in that wild, breathless jump from the top of the falls and as she cast about for them Griff leapt down beside her, cutting her off from the path to the beach. A bubble of panic rose to her throat as he moved slowly towards her, then a flash of orange caught her eye. It was Jack showing her the way and she turned and plunged after him through the thick curtain of vegetation, ignoring Griff's urgent warning shout.

There was a path of sorts — the one she had seen from the top of the falls. It was steep, damp beneath her bare feet, but she didn't care. As she heard Griff at her back she flew down it.

'Maddy, stop!' She half turned and missed the tangle of roots until it was too late and she was already falling and pain was spearing through her ankle. 'Oh, Maddy,' Griff said as he came to a halt beside her. 'What ever am I going to do with you?' he said, tucking down beside her on his haunches.

'Nothing! Stay away from me.' She made a move to stand and for a moment she thought it was going to be all right. She could ignore the pain, she told herself. Then she put her weight on her ankle and she was falling again, this time into Griff's waiting arms, but as everything went black it no longer seemed to matter.

Her faint could not have lasted more than a second or two. She was dimly aware of being carried swiftly along the path in Griff's arms, every step jarring her injured ankle. She gritted her teeth, refusing to cry out. And then, after a hundred yards or so, the elusive scent of the frangipani, which had seemed to haunt her all day, grew steadily stronger until quite suddenly the tree swam into focus beside her, its ugly grey bulbous branches laden with exquisite, scented blossoms.

And there was something else beyond the tree. For a moment she couldn't quite work out what she was looking at, so well was the house disguised from the casual observer. Then she stiffened in disbelief. A house! While she had been living in the most primitive conditions on the beach, civilisation had been a few hundred yards away with hot running water, beds without sand . . .

And not just any house. The wooden roof shingles seemed to mock her; the supporting posts that did nothing to interrupt the cooling breeze might almost have sprung from her own laughing words as she had accepted Griff's invitation to describe the kind of house she would build on this island if it were hers. For a moment the whole idea seemed so ridiculous that she wondered if she might be dreaming, or if the house was a mirage conjured up from a childish game of make-believe by her unconscious brain. She closed her eyes and opened them again. It was still there. And then she remembered his amusement at her description — restrained, under the circumstances.

Maddy looked up into Griff's concerned eyes, then looked away again quickly. 'Very funny,' she snapped.

'I'm not laughing, Maddy,' he said softly.

'Oh, please, don't hold back, Dragon Man, you might split something . . .' She caught her breath as he stepped up onto the veranda and hot pain jarred through her ankle.

'Don't move,' he said as he laid her carefully on a thickly upholstered sofa. 'I'll be right back.'

'Please don't rush,' she told his retreating back through gritted teeth. Then, as she lay back against the soft cushions, she added, 'I'm not going anywhere.'

She stared up at the veranda roof
— a series of pyramid shapes supported
on thick pillars, lined and crossed with
sweetly scented native woods, each
delineating a separate room open to the
breeze blowing in from the sea. Her
first impression of the Dragon Man's
lair had been quite wrong. It went far
beyond her own simple idea of a small
beach house hidden from the world by
the thick forest. This was a masterpiece
of design and construction.

She lay on one of two huge sofas
covered with dark green linen which
were set on either side of a low, square
mahogany table, very old and so thick
that it must have taken four men to
move. Cool rattan chairs were upholstered in tropical shades of green and
yellow. And everywhere there were tall
plants and beautiful *objets d'art*, in
brilliant colours that began to merge
into one.

Then the colour was gone and Griff's
face swam above her and he gently
pushed back the hair that was clinging

limply to her forehead. 'I'm sorry, Maddy,' he said. 'But I'm afraid this is going to hurt.'

★   ★   ★

When Maddy opened her eyes the sky was white and she frowned. That couldn't be right. This was paradise and the sky was always blue.

She moved her head, but it wasn't lying on the sand. It was propped on a soft down pillow. She turned and was immediately aware of a pair of thighs inches from her face. Strong, tanned, impossible to ignore. She gave it her best shot, closing her eyes, but he didn't go away. Instead he laid his hand upon her forehead.

'How are you feeling?'

She stiffened at his touch. 'You really don't want to know that.'

'Sore? Well, I've brought you some painkillers for your ankle.'

'Ankle?' She glanced down at her feet; one of them had been expertly

219

strapped. That wasn't pain. Not real pain.

'I was afraid you'd broken it, but it's just a sprain. Come on, I'll help you up.' Without waiting for her agreement, he hooked his arm under hers and lifted her into a sitting position, propping the pillows behind her. Then he held out a couple of tablets and a glass of water.

'Civilisation as we know it.' But two tablets could do nothing for the pain of treachery so deep that she knew she would rather have been lying on the beach than face the truth.

'Since you fainted on my doorstep, it was easier to bring you here than return you to the beach.'

'The dragon's lair?' For a moment she challenged him, but then stared down at herself, at the unfamiliar bathrobe. 'I was wearing a swimsuit when I fell.'

'A wet, somewhat muddy swimsuit,' he said, with a degree of matter-of-factness for which she knew she should be grateful, but wasn't. 'Would you like something to eat?'

'No. Thank you. I've quite gone off fish.'

His expression warned her that she was pushing her luck. 'What about a cup of tea and a lightly boiled egg?'

It sounded like bliss, but she refused to be so easily tempted. 'China tea?' she enquired, with just a hint of acid. 'And are the eggs free-range?'

His eyes sparked in the soft, cool light of the room. 'For a moment back there, Maddy Rufus, I almost thought you were human.'

For a moment back there, 'Griff will do', I almost believed it myself, Maddy thought, but said nothing.

'Whilst I am in fact a callous, gold-digging little brat who needs a serious lesson in manners?' she enquired. 'I mean why else would we be camping on the beach when you've got a perfectly . . . adequate . . . house?'

'Why else?' he murmured softly.

'Well, you've made your point, Dragon Man. Had your fun. Lesson learned. Now, will you get on the radio and call up someone to take me home, or will I?'

His jaw tightened ominously. 'I can't do that, I'm afraid.' She was almost convinced by that regretful little shrug. 'I've never bothered to install one. I've always used the one on the plane or — '

'Or the yacht?' she demanded. How much more was she going to have to bear? 'Where is it?'

'On charter for the next month. It's not a toy; it has to earn its keep. Sorry.'

'You're not in the least bit sorry,' she stormed. 'You're enjoying yourself. Just wait until I tell Zoe — '

His face darkened. 'I was beginning to enjoy myself,' he said tersely. 'The bathroom's through there, so if you don't need my help . . . ?'

'I'm sure I can manage.' She stood up to demonstrate that she needed nothing from him. Absolutely nothing. 'My ankle isn't that bad.'

'Ah, well, you see, I did a first-aid

course once . . . You never know when it might come in useful.' And he shut the door with a snap as he left the room.

Maddy blinked as tears stung at her lids. It would be ridiculous to cry. She never cried. At least, for years and years. She stared determinedly about her, trying very hard not to think about him undressing her. She was in an enormous room, the stark whiteness of the walls broken only by two very beautiful primitive paintings the brilliant colours of which vibrated against the dark masculine furniture.

And the bathroom was enormous, with simple blue and white tiles and dark mahogany fittings. There was a shower, a bath big enough for two and a pile of dark blue plush towels exactly like the one he had used on the beach. Not Zoe's, then. Had he come and collected it so that she would be more comfortable lying on the sand? 'Oh, Maddy, wake up, girl. It wasn't meant for you. You were meant to lie on the sand and suffer,' she told herself. If she hadn't had hysterics, she would undoubtedly have done just that instead of spending the night wrapped in the safety of his arms. She stared at her reflection in the mirror. Her tan had darkened a shade or two, her hair was, if anything even brighter after a couple of days spent outside, but nothing else had changed. Not on the outside.

She removed the robe and sponged herself all over with warm water and was drying herself when she heard the bedroom door open. Wrapping the towel around her like a sarong, she hopped to the bathroom door. 'Is this accommodation temporary,' she demanded, 'or can I have my bags?'

'Say please and anything's possible.'

'I'd rather sleep — '

'Say and it's a fact!' he warned.

'In my own nightdress,' she said, rapidly retreating from her threat, certain that he wasn't bluffing. 'And I need a toothbrush.'

'They'll wait. Come and have something to eat.'

'Dressed like this?'

'I promise you, Maddy, no one is about to call.' And he held the bedroom door wide, inviting her out onto the terrace.

She threw the end of the towel over her shoulder and made to sweep by him, for the moment forgetting her ankle. He caught her as the pain took her unawares, and picked her up.

'Keep your hands off me,' she demanded, trying to shake free of him.

'This is my house, Maddy Osborne, and I'm the only one who gives orders in it.'

'You are nothing but a . . . a . . . '

'Lost for words?' he enquired.

'I'm too much of a lady to utter them.'

'I know what I am, Maddy Rufus,' he told her. 'The jury's still out on you.' Before she could reply he carried her to the table, sitting her on one of the high-backed chairs before which had been laid the promised eggs, a pile of fresh toast and a pot of tea. Despite the fact that the sun was already turning the sky pink and it was hours since she had eaten, she ignored them, fixing her gaze instead upon the table. It was cut from a single cross-section of some richly dappled gold and brown timber and supported on crossed legs of a much darker wood.

'You have excellent taste in furniture,' she said, studiously ignoring the eggs. 'Did some local craftsman make this for you?'

'I made it and when you've got a spare month I'll tell you about it. Right now I want you to eat.'

'I'm not hungry,' she said, regarding him with the stubborn expression that had once made teachers quake. Griff was unmoved.

He caught her wrist and put a spoon into her hand. 'Force yourself,' he said with quiet authority, and sank to his haunches so that his eyes were on a level with hers.

'I'm not hungry,' she insisted, trying to keep her own voice on the same even keel as his, but she knew that another minute of the tantalising smell of fresh toast would drive her stomach to noisy reproach. She tugged at her wrist, but although his grasp was light it was not to be moved. Besides, his eyes were inescapable; they pinned her to the chair like a butterfly to a card.

'Now,' he continued in the same quiet voice, 'I'm going to fetch your bag from the plane. But just so you don't misunderstand my determination I'm going to tell you what I will do if you defy me.' Apprehension cartwheeled beneath her ribs. There was something very ominous about his insistence.

'What?' Her voice caught drily in her throat, but she lifted her chin a little. 'What will you do?'

He lifted the towel where it was draped over her naked shoulder and ran the edge of his thumb along her collar-bone. She shivered convulsively and he nodded as if satisfied. 'If, when I return, you haven't eaten every scrap I shall remove this very fetching sarong and make love to you, Maddy. Right here.'

8

There was no emotion, no threatening gesture. The words were completely matter-of-fact. He might just as easily have said, I'll have a cup of tea and a biscuit. Yet she believed him. It was frightening how easy he was to believe. More terrifying still was the way her body kindled to his threat.

'On the dining table?'

'Whatever turns you on.'

'But . . . that would be rape,' she replied hoarsely.

'No.' He finally released her wrist and raised his hand to her face. The pad of his thumb grazed the hot flare of colour on her cheekbones and a little shock wave rippled beneath her skin, fanning out from the epicentre of his touch until her body felt consumed, her mind unravelling in her desire for him. He offered a sympathetic smile as if he understood. 'Not rape, Maddy. It would be much worse than that. We both know that you'd be begging for more.' He uncurled in one graceful movement and walked away.

Fear so raw that she could taste it rippled through her and she looked at the spoon still clasped in her hand. She wanted to smash the egg with it. Instead, she began to tap the egg, very gently, removing the shell in the slow, meticulous manner that she had once used to drive her mother to fury and that in some subtle way defied him. But nevertheless she ate it all, and every crumb of toast, although it practically stuck in her throat. Because, no matter how much she denied it to herself, she knew she was in no position to call his bluff. How could such a thing have happened? How could she have fallen in love with him when she believed him to be her worst nightmare? And there was still the cheque.

He had not returned by the time she finished and, refusing to sit like a child waiting for permission to leave the table, she gathered the dishes and hobbled painfully to the kitchen with them.

The kitchen was decorated in an earthy mixture of pale terracotta, soft creams and rich dark wood. Perfect, like the rest of the house. But she didn't want to think about the house, because that meant thinking about the way he had deceived her. She quickly filled the sink with warm water and washed up, leaning against the edge of the unit to take the weight of her foot. It didn't take long.

She made her way slowly back to the terrace, determined to put her foot up on one of the sofas, but then it occurred to her that she would never have a better opportunity to look around. Despite his casual denial of a radio, it seemed unlikely that a man in Griff's position would be so cavalier about communications. He would surely have some backup? She grasped the handle of a tantalisingly closed door and began to turn it. Then she stopped. He'd had his fun at her expense. It was over. Why on earth would he pretend?

★ ★ ★

'Griff?'

She found him contemplating the inlet a few yards from the little seaplane. It was the first time she had voluntarily spoken to him for three days — three long days during which there had been no sign of a search for them by air or sea and Maddy's nerves had been stretched to breaking-point by the almost unbearable intimacy of sharing a house with him.

'Maddy?' he replied with a laconic lift of a brow, and she almost winced.

She had known it would not be easy, but she couldn't let things drift on like this and she had screwed herself to the sticking-point to face his amusement that she had finally been forced to beg. But it was as clear as day that Griff was content to continue as they were — swimming in the calm water of the inlet and idling their time away. It was as if he was waiting for something. And this was, after all, his home. He was doing precisely what he'd intended to do — fish a little, read, explore the reef with a snorkel. She had watched, wanting to accept his casual invitations to join him, but unwilling to risk the flare of damped-down passion that she was so intensely aware was just beneath the surface.

'We can't go on like this.'

'I can,' he assured her, but as her eyes pleaded with him to understand he relented and patted the sand beside him. 'Sit down. Tell me what's on your mind.'

'You know what's on my mind,' she said, ignoring his invitation to sit. 'I want to get off this island and go home.'

'Really? I thought it was imperative that you stay with Zoe?'

'That was Father's idea. He thought . . .'

233

It didn't matter what he thought. Whatever Zoe's cheque was for, it clearly wasn't to support the Dragon Man in idleness. 'Once I'm off this island I'm getting the first available flight back to London. My father will be going frantic, not having heard from me.'

He looked up at her, shading his eyes from the sun. 'You do know, then, that people worry about you?'

She frowned slightly. 'Of course I do.'

'I didn't mean the fact that you are long overdue on your visit to Zoe's.'

'Didn't you?' What else could he mean? Then she brushed his interruption away with an irritable little twitch of her hand. 'Anyway, Zoe clearly hasn't been all that bothered . . . ' She went suddenly cold as a shiver ran down her spine. 'Unless . . . ' She looked at him. 'Unless they think we crashed into the sea. That we're . . . ' She covered her hand with her mouth and sank onto the sand beside him, forgetting her anger with him in her anguish. 'That's it, isn't it? That's why the authorities aren't looking for us. They think we're dead.' She stuffed her fist into her mouth. 'Dad will have to go to Paris to tell my mother . . . ' He wouldn't telephone and despite everything, he still loved her too much to let anyone else do it. She felt tears of pity for them both well up in her eyes. 'Oh, Griff. This is awful.'

He swore softly and put his arm around her, thumbing away the tears that had unaccountably welled onto her cheeks. 'Oh, come on; it isn't that bad.'

She looked up at him. Why wouldn't he understand? 'Griff, this is serious . . . '

'If anyone thought we were in trouble they'd be out looking for wreckage, Maddy. Zoe probably thinks I've tempted you to my lair and is being terribly discreet.'

'She would never think that!'

His brows rose sharply at her indignant denial. 'My mistake.' Then he frowned. 'I thought you said you didn't have a mother.'

Maddy remembered with painful

clarity exactly what she had said to him: I no longer have a mother. She had thought it for so long that she hadn't realised how heartless, how cruel it was until this moment when she pictured her mother grieving for her. She had blamed her for so much ... 'My mother left, years ago.'

'Another man?'

She shook her head. 'No. She has her faults, but faithlessness isn't one of them.'

'Then what?'

'Money.'

'Ah, the Osborne family failing.'

'My mother certainly thought so. When she discovered that Dad had mortgaged the house for the fifth time to finance his latest venture she just walked out. She couldn't take the fear any more, I suppose. Dad had come close to disaster before and she'd lost her home when everything had had to be sold to pay men's wages and the creditors.'

'But you didn't go with her?'

'Someone had to stay and look after Dad. Perhaps daughters are less critical than wives.'

'But you blamed her?' He saw everything so clearly, so black and white. But he was right. She did blame her mother that she had been left to cook and clean and answer the telephone and be her father's unpaid secretary when she should have been working for her A levels. You didn't walk out on your responsibilities. She had scraped through her exams with the bare minimum, and instead of accomplishing her dream of reading English at Oxford she had ended up doing a year at a local college.

Maddy discovered that she was smiling at the irony of it. An English degree might just have got her a job in a publishing house. Business studies had given her the foundation to run a successful company of her own. Life had its own pattern. One door closed and another opened.

'Maddy?' She realised that he was

waiting for an answer.

'Living with him must have been a nightmare for someone like my mother, who loves order and security. The pity of it was that after all those years of worrying whether she was going to be able to pay the electricity bill he had made his first million within a year of her leaving.'

'I'm surprised she didn't come back. Or perhaps she felt guilty about leaving you?'

Maddy hadn't thought about it clearly for a long time. Now she shook her head. 'If you only knew half the things she had to put up with . . . '

'Perhaps you should tell her how you feel.'

She looked at him then. 'Perhaps I should.' It was like a door opening in her heart and she smiled. 'And when I open the Paris branch I'll be able to spend a lot more time with her.'

'The Paris branch?' The irony was back.

She gave an apologetic little shrug.

'Like father, like daughter. I shall have to raise the money on my flat if I decide to go ahead. It must run in the blood.'

'Unless you can catch a rich husband in the meantime?'

Maddy met Griff's eye and gave a little shiver. 'That will do it every time,' she conceded sarcastically. Considering that she wasn't supposed to be talking to the man, it occurred to Maddy that this conversation seemed to have got rather out of hand. She had rehearsed what she was going to say to him. The bare minimum. How had they ever got so far off the subject? She disengaged herself from the comforting curve of his arm. 'But to snare the prize I have to get off this island.'

'You want me to build a raft?' he offered.

She remembered the table. 'Could you do that?'

'It would take a while,' he said with a shrug. 'Have you ever tried to saw up palm wood with your teeth?'

'No, I haven't,' she said, leaping to

her feet, cross with herself for falling so easily for his teasing.

'You have something more practical in mind? A message in a bottle, perhaps?'

She glared at him. 'I'm not prepared to sit here any longer and do nothing.'

He linked his fingers behind his head, lay back on the sand and closed his eyes. 'You should try it once in a while, Maddy. You might enjoy it.'

She allowed her eyes to make a lingering journey down the strong column of his neck, across a pair of well-muscled shoulders and the deep chest with its scattering of body hair that arrowed to a fine dark line across his taut hips. He had confounded her theory that he lacked a bathing suit, but the black slip that hugged his hips did very little to disguise his manhood and the skin across her high cheekbones darkened. Oh, she could enjoy it. Despite her frantic attempts to keep busy with sketching, taking photographs, teaching Jack some new words — anything to occupy her mind — she knew that if things had been different between them she would have been more than happy to lie back and . . . She jerked her gaze away to find that he had opened his eyes and was watching her.

'It's time for the last resort, Griff. I want you to set fire to the plane,' she said, wanting to shock him, provoke some reaction other than a cool, teasing smile. He didn't move. 'I'll pay you if that's what it takes. How much is that old plane worth?' Not by one twitch of a muscle did he betray that he had understood what she was demanding. 'The smoke will be black, acrid.' The words began to tumble out as he still made no response, but his eyes hardened. 'Not like a bonfire. It would be seen from the other islands. It couldn't be ignored.'

'No,' he agreed, 'it certainly couldn't be ignored. I'm sure we'd be descended upon by every environmental officer in the Grenadines and beyond, all demanding to know why we were polluting the atmosphere.'

'It's an emergency!'

'Really? You've been delayed a few days and it's a crisis? Everyone must jump to attention?'

'I want to get away from you, Griff. And you needn't pretend you'd be desolated to lose this particular Eve.'

'Maybe I would. After all, you have a certain entertainment value.'

'Entertainment value?' She could hardly believe her ears. 'I hardly dare ask . . . ?'

'I particularly like the way you curl your tongue over your lip when you're concentrating very hard.'

'I don't!'

'You do, actually. And that little wriggle you give before you fling yourself into the sea.' He moved his hand to demonstrate. 'And those black stockings — '

'All right,' she said quickly. 'You can set me up as a public amusement and charge admittance if you'll just get me off this island!'

He shrugged. 'It's a lot to ask, Maddy.'

'Well, if you'd made more of an effort — ' She stopped, began again a little more placatingly this time. 'I know it's probably your pride and joy, Griff, but — '

He lifted his head to look at her. 'You haven't much time for other people's feelings, have you, Maddy?'

She stared at him. 'And just what is that supposed to mean?'

'What do you think all this has been about?' She stared at him. 'Cast your mind back a few days and put yourself in the shoes of Mr Rupert Hartnoll.'

'Rupert?' she demanded. 'What on earth has he got to do with you? Are you life-long buddies or something?'

'I've never met the man.'

'I congratulate you,' she said.

'You told me yourself that he asked you to marry him. You're not suggesting you offered him no encouragement?'

'I'm not suggesting anything,' Maddy replied, as angry with herself for her uncharitable remark as with Griff for provoking it. Rupert had been the most charming companion until he had suddenly decided that she would make him the perfect wife. 'It was none of your business.'

'I made it my business. Tell me about 'real' money, Maddy Rufus,' he said, recalling for her the jibe she'd made to Rupert at the villa. 'What would it take to buy your heart? Or have you got one?' He regarded her stonily. 'Or is it just a cash register that rings when a man with sufficient cash bears his soul?'

Once. Once she had had a heart and for the briefest moment in Griff's arms she'd begun to think that it might be resuscitated. 'I don't want to talk about it.'

His eyes gleamed coldly. 'If you want me to set fire to my plane, I'm afraid you're going to have to.'

'Damn you, Griff. I'll do it myself!' She turned to walk away but his hand snapped around her ankle strapping, detaining her. 'Let go of me,' she gasped, unable to pull away.

'I thought you'd need this.' He was

turning the lighter between the fingers of his other hand. Maddy made a wild grab for it and collapsed to the sand as her foot gave beneath her.

'Give it to me,' she demanded, but he held it away from her.

'Not before you tell me all about your poor rejected lover.'

She was sprawled across him and his questing eyes were boring uncomfortably into her. She sat up quickly, putting a little space between them. 'Why should I tell you anything?' she asked, a little huskily. She wanted the lighter, but she didn't see why she should indulge his curiosity.

'Let's say I'm a student of human nature,' he said. 'And I'm giving you the opportunity to tell me your side of the story.'

Why was he so insistent? Why on earth did he care about one rejected suitor, a man he had never even met? 'Rupert Hartnoll isn't poor and he was never my lover. Just obsessed . . . I didn't realise quite how badly until he turned up in Mustique and persuaded my father to let him stay with us.'

'Not poor? Not rich enough for you, though — '

'*Real* money, for your information, Griff, is a family code, a joke between Dad and me. It's the kind of money you earn yourself. Like my father, like me. Like . . . like you. Two pounds or two million pounds. The amount is immaterial.'

She saw him frown as he digested this information. 'But surely it doesn't matter — ?'

'Doesn't it? Since Dad's become successful we've met a lot of people with the unreal kind — people like Rupert. He has a whole bankful, inherited from generations of Hartnolls who never dirtied their hands with the stuff but employed clever people to make more and more for them. People like my father. But he broke free . . . took unbelievable risks to be his own man.' She surged on before he could interrupt. 'Rupert is good-looking, charming and, despite anything unkind I've said, he can be great company when he isn't imagining himself in love. But charm is not enough.'

'Not even charm and money?'

'A man has to have more than that, surely? If Rupert lost all he had tomorrow he wouldn't know how to earn the money to buy himself a loaf of bread. He certainly wouldn't be able to live off the land.'

'I see.' Did he? Had she betrayed herself? She glanced swiftly at him, wondering if he had caught her unintentional reference to his ability to live at ease with the world, but his eyes gave nothing away.

But Maddy had gone too far, exposed more of herself than she had ever intended and she felt the need to disguise her heart. 'Of course,' she said, with a little toss of her head, 'his grandmother's ghastly ruby and diamond cluster ring was the last straw. I mean, with my colouring . . . '

He caught a wayward strand and

wrapped it around his fingers. 'I can see that he should have made the effort to choose something more suitable,' he said gravely. 'Something rare, individual — '

'It wouldn't have made any difference,' she said, regaining control of her hair and tucking it firmly behind her ears.

'Because of the money?'

'Because I didn't love him.' Silence greeted this reply. Finally she had said something that he couldn't respond to with some sarcastic remark. 'May I have the lighter, Griff?' she asked, after an age.

He seemed to come from a long way off and snapped his hand shut over the lighter. 'Some things in this world are beyond price. Rupert Hartnoll could not buy your love, Maddy,' he said. 'And not even *real* money can buy my plane.' As if to emphasise this, he tucked the lighter back in the top of his briefs, tantalisingly within reach, but far too dangerously placed to risk . . .

'I'll see you get another one,' she said

urgently. 'At least as good. Better.'

'No, Maddy. You see, it's irreplaceable; it's part of what makes me what I am.'

'And what are you?' She jumped to her feet. 'You criticise me for being callous, but there'll be people out there grieving for you too. Haven't you got a thought in your head for them?'

'A wailing and a gnashing of pretty white teeth all over the Caribbean?' he offered, so perilously close to her own thoughts that she felt quite naked. He smiled as if he knew, and added, 'Just think of the party when I return from the dead.'

'Damn you!' She stamped. It was a mistake and before she could recover he was up and beside her, his arm about her waist, and she was so close to him that she could feel the hard shape of the lighter pressed against her waist.

'You once boasted that there was nothing wrong with your manners,' he said, with a savage little smile. 'My plane may not be for sale, but if you'd remembered to say please I might just have given it away.' The sensuous curve of his mouth was inches from her own, his thigh hard and warm against her own, and despite everything a tremor of desire warned her that this was a trap. He touched her cheek, grazing it lightly with his knuckles. 'Say please, Maddy, and you can take the lighter . . . if you dare.'

'Go to hell!' And she stepped back, pushing him away with the flat of her palms, and he made no effort to hold her as she hobbled away.

But that night she ignored the food he cooked for her. He could do what he wanted; she just wasn't hungry. She crawled miserably into bed and contemplated another night, another day in a paradise that seemed tantalisingly within reach, a paradise to which she was unable to find the key.

★ ★ ★

She slept fitfully, dreaming uneasily of her mother — that calm, serene woman who had rejected her husband's love because he had wanted excitement, risk. Maddy began to shout at her, tell her she was crazy, stupid, that nothing was perfect, that she must take what life offered. But her mother couldn't hear and she was drifting further and further away. 'No!' Maddy cried. 'No! Come back!'

'Maddy!' Griff was holding her, crushing her against his chest as she reached out for her mother. 'It was just a dream, my love. Hush now.' He captured her arms and turned her into him, rocking her gently, and gradually she stopped struggling, became aware of her surroundings, the large white bedroom. That he was holding her. That he had called her his love.

'A dream?' she murmured. What was dream and what was fact?

He brushed the hair back from her face. 'Do you want to talk about it?'

She shook her head, then realised what he meant. 'It was my mother. I haven't dreamed about her for a long time.'

'You'll see her soon.'

'Will I? It doesn't seem very likely.'

'I promise.' He regarded the tangled, damp ruin of her bed. 'Come on. You can't stay here. You can have my bed — '

'No, I'll be all right,' she said quickly, pulling back.

'Don't argue.'

'I can't . . .'

'I hadn't planned to share it with you, Maddy.'

'Why would you?' She shook her head. 'It's just that I don't want to go back to sleep. Dreams sometimes come back — '

'Then we'll go down to the beach and wait for the sunrise.' He lifted her from the bed and, cradling her in his arms, carried her down the path to the white crescent of the beach, settling beside her, cradling her head against his shoulder.

'Another day in paradise,' she said with a sigh.

'It could be.'

'Not for me.'

'Try a little harder. Listen.' The sea lapped gently against the shore to the counterpoint of tree frogs chirping in the forest and the occasional disgruntled chuntering of a bird disturbed on its perch. ' 'A ship, an isle, a sickle moon — /With few but with how splendid stars/The mirrors of the sea are strewn/Between their silver bars!' '

Maddy turned to Griff, her cheek brushing against his shoulder as she looked up into his face. 'That's beautiful.'

In the moon's deep shadows he seemed to smile. 'It's a pity that the moon's full. Perhaps I could tempt you back when it's new.'

'Tempt me? Don't you know that if you wanted me, Griff, I'd never go away?'

'Want you?' He groaned softly. 'Maddy, don't you know how much I want you? Why else would I care what you are, what you do — ?'

It was enough. She laid a finger to

his lips. 'Don't speak. Don't say anything.' And when she was sure that he would obey she took her hand away, replacing that light touch with her lips, kissing him, softly, gently as the sigh of the waves, and in that moment her body seemed as fragile as an eggshell — his to cradle gently in his hand, or to break.

'Oh, Maddy,' he breathed as her head fell back across his arm to expose her smooth white throat. 'You idiot. You crazy, beautiful little idiot.' Then he buried his face in her neck, his mouth firing a trail of kisses across that delicate arch, his tongue liquid fire as it traced the sensitive hollow of her collar-bone, and his hands slid beneath the baggy T-shirt she had worn for sleeping, to cradle her back, the pads of his fingers deliciously rough against her skin, sending tiny shivers of electricity charging through her veins.

Maddy reached out tentatively, to stroke her fingertips through the rough hair of his naked chest, to graze small male nipples that hardened to her wondering touch, and she felt almost giddy with the heady sense of power as he trembled beneath her hands.

'Maddy!' He gasped an urgent warning. 'I'm not made of wood.' As if to demonstrate his all too potent humanity, he lifted up the T-shirt, drawing it over her head, dropping it to the sand. Maddy, her arms upraised as if in supplication to the moon, its rays shimmering her body with silver, felt only gratitude for her release, the glorious sense of freedom. The most gentle of breezes rippled from the inlet, stirring her hair, cooling her fevered skin, and she couldn't wait to be completely naked. She uncurled from the sand like a nymph, standing for one breathless second before Griff's kneeling figure.

'Help me, Griff,' she said from somewhere deep in her throat, in a voice she barely recognised as her own.

'Oh, dear God, Maddy,' he groaned, laying his cheek against the soft curve of her belly, his hands cupping the flare of her hips. 'You don't know what you're doing to me.'

She looked down and touched his face, traced the outline of his cheekbone, his jaw, the warm, soft curve of his lips that parted and caught her fingertips. In that moment when they were on the brink, when sanity was still — just — a possibility, she understood with an almost blinding clarity of vision that no matter what else she did with the rest of her life this was one moment that she would never regret.

'Show me.' Her voice quickened. 'Show me what I'm doing to you.'

Griff slipped his hands beneath the silk wisp of her panties and suddenly she was exultantly free, standing before him, ready for love as she had never been in her life. His lips touched the delicate white skin in the hollow of her hips and her whole body shivered with the shock of pleasure, her bones melting as his mouth, his tongue, his hands traversed her body, rising with almost agonising slowness across the plane of her stomach, exploring the indentation of her navel, the curve of her waist.

He rose to his feet then to wonder at the soft swell of her breast, drawing each firm tip into his mouth to tease it with the tip of his tongue, his teeth, until she was moaning softly deep in her throat, her nails digging into his shoulders as she thought she might pass out from the exquisite, almost agonising pleasure. Then he raised his head.

'Now it's your turn, Maddy,' he said, his voice scorching her skin.

Hardly knowing where to begin, she could only follow her instinct and the lead he had given, using her hands, her tongue to explore his body, wanting to give as much pleasure as he had given her, and taking it in the little involuntary shivers and moans of delight that her untutored touch provoked from him. And when she encountered the barrier of his shorts she did not hesitate but slipped the button at his waist.

Then, with fingers that trembled as the velvet hardness of his need for her became demandingly apparent, she released him, shaking from head to toe as she eased the cloth over his hips. But her need was as strong as his and as his shorts fell away she slid her hands beneath his buttocks and pulled him against her.

'Love me, Griff,' she breathed, and there was a roaring in her ears that might have been some primeval male love call, or might have been her own fierce need pounding through her veins. Whatever. It didn't matter. His mouth was urgent as his lips claimed hers and they sank together onto the damp sand, and with only the warm night air to cover them and the waves lapping at their thighs he carried her with him to some glorious height from which they finally plunged in a wild, reckless fall that echoed that dizzy leap from the lip of the waterfall. For a moment she was utterly, gloriously breathless. Then, laughing at the sheer, unexpected glory of it, Maddy looked up at him. 'Would you like to go back and do that again?' she asked.

He stared down into her face, a little crease of concern drawing his brows together. 'Maddy . . .'

She raised her hand to touch the frown, smooth it away. 'Don't look so serious.'

'It's just that you took me by surprise. I didn't expect . . . It's been a while, since you've had a lover?'

She felt a little stab of pain. 'Did I disappoint you?'

'Don't you know?' he whispered.

'I thought . . . it seemed . . .' She tried to read his face, but it was all shadows. 'I know that I'm not very good . . .'

'Dear God, you don't know,' he murmured, and she felt foolish, unbearably young and inexperienced.

She struggled to sit up, attempting to move away from him, but his hands captured her, held her. 'I'm sorry if I disappointed you — '

259

'Disappointed? I feel . . . ' Laughter bubbled from low in his throat. 'I feel like the first man on earth.' And he kissed her with such painful tenderness that she could not doubt him, and finally, when the need for air drove them apart, her breath caught on a little sob of happiness and tears spilled down her cheeks.

'Tell me, Maddy,' he demanded fiercely. She shook her head, not wanting to destroy the perfection of the moment with dark thoughts of the past. 'Tell me who hurt you that much.' When she would have pulled away, he refused to let her go. 'Don't let it poison your life, Maddy. Talk about it.'

'I wouldn't know where to start,' she mumbled into his chest. It was so long since she had allowed herself even to think about it.

'Start with his name.'

His name. 'Andrew.' Her voice was so faint that she could scarcely hear it herself. She met Griff's clear, penetrating eyes and drew strength from him.

'His name was Andrew,' she said, more bravely, and after that it seemed to pour out — the glamour of a man five years her senior, with a minor title, a job in the city and a sleek red sports car. And the family estate in Gloucestershire. Every young girl's dream.

'How old were you?'

'Just nineteen.' A very protected, rather naïve nineteen, fresh from a college course, with her heart and everything else intact and worlds to conquer. And her father's sudden wealth had meant that it was a much larger world than anything she had been used to. Without her mother to act as his hostess she had been pitchforked headlong into it. She plucked at the sand, unwilling to relive her humiliation.

9

'Tell me, Maddy.'

'I ... I can't. I've never told anyone ...'

He took her chin in his hand and turned her to face him. 'You will tell me.' His voice was gentle, but there was an insistence, a firmness about his mouth that could not be denied.

And Maddy discovered that despite the pain of recalling that dreadful awakening from innocence she did want to tell him. 'I was young enough to be bowled over by his eagerness to marry me. He'd actually got the licence in his pocket and wanted to whisk me away to the nearest register office.'

'What stopped him?'

'I was stubbornly dewy-eyed. I wanted a white wedding in church with a dozen bridesmaids and all my family and friends. That needed more than a few days to organise, and my father's cheque-book to pay for it. And Dad insisted we waited six months.' Although, being wise in the ways of the world, he'd suggested it would be a good idea to go on the Pill. 'In the meantime I was invited down to Gloucester to meet the family, get to know them.'

'No doubt they rolled out the red carpet.'

She felt a warmth at the fact that he had so quickly understood. 'Red carpet, antique crystal, grandmother's ring . . . ' Her voice quavered on that.

'Rubies?'

'I scarcely noticed, I was so happy.'

'And with Grandma's ring on your finger Andrew decided it was high time to cement the relationship? I'm sure you had conveniently adjoining rooms?'

'Not adjoining. My bag was in his room. I was surprised, in his parents' home . . . but he said they would expect it . . . After all, we were engaged . . . and they were miles away on the other side of the house . . . '

'I'm sure he was very convincing.' Griff said abruptly, refusing to allow her to dwell on it. 'How did you find out that he was after your money?'

'We'd been out to lunch and afterwards he wanted to go back to his flat . . . I found his constant desire for me . . . reassuring. I knew I wasn't very good . . . '

Griff swore somewhere deep under his breath. 'You are breathtaking.'

She shook her head as if she still could not believe him. 'When we got in the light was flashing on the answering machine. He switched it on as he walked past and went across the room to fortify himself with a drink before the coming ordeal . . . ' She faltered. 'Anyway, he was too far away to stop it when the first message was so obviously something I shouldn't hear . . . It was his father, wanting to know how much longer it was going to take his son to get one stupid girl pregnant.' She stared at the sand. 'Apparently they were one step away from the bankruptcy court and I had been elected for the privilege of bailing them out. I'd never heard such crude language. Although, I discovered very swiftly that it ran in the family. When I told Andrew that I had been taking the Pill he seemed to take great pleasure in explaining in graphic detail just how tedious I was in bed.'

'Nasty,' Griff said tightly.

She couldn't begin to describe how nasty it had been. 'It could have been a lot . . . nastier. If I hadn't found out . . . '

He lifted her hand to his lips. 'I'm deeply flattered that you trusted me enough . . . I still can't believe it. You're beautiful, so utterly desirable . . . '

'Don't stop,' she said, her voice shaking on a tiny hiccup.

He grinned. 'Provoking, irritating, impetuous . . . '

She flung herself across him. 'Has anyone ever told you that you talk too much?'

'You have the cure in your own hands — ' He broke off to moan disjointedly as she took him at his word and began to torment him with delicate caresses. 'Maddy, please . . . please . . . '

'Hands don't seem to work,' she murmured then gave a little scream as he rolled over and pinned her beneath him.

'Perhaps you'd better leave it to me.'

'Please . . . ' she begged. 'Once more before the moon goes down. We may be rescued tomorrow.'

'Don't you know, my darling, that tomorrow never comes?'

'If only that were true . . . '

'It is. You have my word.' And the reassurance of his lips was all the promise she would ever need.

* * *

They didn't see the moon set. But as the first rays of dawn blushed the edge of the sea Griff rose, pulling her up with him in one smooth movement from the sand, swinging her into his arms.

She put her arms about his neck and

laid her cheek against his chest. 'Where are you taking me?'

'Wait, my darling. Just wait for the magic.'

It was still dark in the forest, but he was sure-footed on the path and helped her up the waterfall, holding her close as they stood above the spray, listening to the songbirds call in the canopy high above them to a rising sun they could not see. Beside him, the milky moon flowers were still open, filling the air with their sweetness.

'Maddy.' He breathed her name and kissed her, too briefly. Then he turned her to face the morning as, without warning, the sky blushed, touching the spray from the waterfall, the moonflowers, the surface of the pool, until it seemed to Maddy that the whole world was the most delicate shade of pink. 'Now,' he said, and they leapt together off the end of the world.

When they surfaced, it was over. The early-morning light filtering through the trees was mint-fresh and clear. The droplets of water clung to Griff's hair as his arms slid about her waist and he drew her close.

'Dear heaven,' she whispered as her core turned to liquid desire and her arms linked around his neck, drawing him down to her. 'What have you done to me?' But as they slid together beneath the water, wrapped in each other's arms, there was no answer and Maddy no longer cared.

They exploded to the surface and she turned and ducked away from him, but her throaty laugh invited chase and they swam like a pair of young otters, hardly aware whether they were under the water or breathing air, their bodies teasing and touching, together, then apart. When Griff caught her, he held her close, possessing her with his lips, his hands, until they were forced upwards once more for air and once more she slipped away, eluding him as he searched for her in the dark water.

Laughing, she caught him from behind, gripping his shoulders and forcing him under, but it had been far too easy. He rolled and took her down with him and this time when he held her prisoner against him there was no escape, nor did she seek one. They hung suspended in time and space, his lips on hers and his tongue exploring her mouth with an exquisite thoroughness until she thought she must dissolve, become a part of him, and Maddy knew that was what she desired most in the entire world.

Then he lifted her from the water and set her on the smooth ledge below the falls. 'Good morning, Maddy Rufus.'

'Good morning, 'Griff will do',' she said shakily, scarcely able to believe what had happened to her in the space of one night. No. Not in one night. The fuse had been lit the moment they'd first set eyes on one another — a long, slow fuse that last night had finally detonated. He put his arm about her and they walked slowly back to the house.

'I'd like to have a shower and wash my hair,' she said as they reached the bedroom door.

'On your own?'

'Do you mind?'

His eyes danced at her blush. 'I think I'm going to hate every moment you're out of my sight.' He kissed her briefly, as if to linger would make leaving too hard.

'Griff . . . ' He glanced back at her, a question in his eyes. But she held back. She mustn't say anything stupid, do anything that would spoil the moment. He held out his arms and she went to him, because despite her need to be alone to take out all these new feelings and examine them she was suddenly afraid to let him go. 'Stay if you want to.'

He dropped a kiss on the top of her head. 'Goose. Go and get under a hot shower; you're shivering. There's something I have to do.' He turned her round, gave her a little slap on the rump and closed the door behind her.

She went into the bathroom and stepped under the shower, but when she reached for the shampoo it was empty. Griff would have some in his bathroom. She left the water running and wrapped the towel around her and stepped onto the veranda. She could smell coffee brewing in the kitchen and smiled. No need to bother him. She padded swiftly on bare feet to his room a few doors away, but froze as she heard his voice raised against the static of a radio . . . A radio.

'Zoe, my darling, I think I can guarantee that she's got the message.' There was a pause. 'We'll fly out today.' He laughed softly. 'I knew you would forgive me; I only hope Maddy will be as generous when she finds out that I faked that emergency landing . . . '

Zoe? Did she know? Was she part of the 'lesson'? And now he was chatting to her as if nothing had happened beyond a few cold showers, a little discomfort. Her heart screamed out to her godmother, Don't listen to him. He

271

has betrayed you, betrayed us both. But guilt kept her silent. It wasn't just Griff who had betrayed Zoe. When she had been wrapped in his arms she hadn't given her godmother a second thought. He had stopped speaking, clearly interrupted, and his shadow disappeared as he moved away from the shuttered window, and she heard the creak of cane as he sank into a chair and when he spoke again his voice was too low to hear what he was saying. But he had said enough.

'One day you'll meet someone who won't take no for an answer,' he had said. She had mocked him and he had wreaked his revenge. All he had had to do was wait and she had fallen like a ripe plum into his lap. It was over. He had won and now he was going to fly her out. Fly her out!

Maddy, her hand still stopping the scream that was clamouring somewhere deep inside her, backed quietly away from the door. She didn't even bother to turn off the shower but dressed in the first thing that came into her hand, grabbed her handbag and fled.

She wasn't certain how she made it to the beach. She could never afterwards recall retracing her steps, only that she'd made it somehow.

Her trembling fingers struggled with the knot that fastened the guy-rope to the palm tree. It wouldn't budge and, terrified that he would discover she was missing and come looking for her, Maddy seized the machete and swung furiously at the rope, slicing it through. The tide was still coming in and she had to wait agonising moments until the seaplane rose on an incoming wave and drifted obligingly out into the bay. She waded after it and climbed on trembling legs into the cockpit. The keys, she knew, were still in the ignition — far the safest place; after all, no one was about to steal a plane that couldn't fly, were they? Certainly not a tease of a girl who needed a serious lesson in how to behave . . .

The engine caught first time, the

propeller biting the air, spinning eagerly, flashing against the sun until it settled into an even rhythm, and suddenly the trembling stopped. She was back in control. The madness had passed and a blissful numbness was, for the moment, blocking the pain as she concentrated on the controls of a strange aircraft. Maddy turned the machine to face the sea, picking up the radio handset to call the tower at Mustique, doing the fastest preflight check in history.

That she had never flown a seaplane before didn't daunt her in the least. It was a simple machine, the controls, on inspection, proving almost identical to those of the plane on which she had learned to fly. In a kind of icy calm she taxied out into the bay and waited for her instructions on height and heading with every outward appearance of calm, concentrating totally on the machine, impervious to Griff's frantic calls as he pounded along the beach.

Her hand trembled slightly as he began to splash through the surf towards her, but she tightened her grip, and as clearance rattled through the static she opened the throttle and pulled back on the control stick, sending the little plane rocketing towards the open sea with the total indifference of someone who knew that nothing could ever get worse. Then, as she saw the white line of surf that betrayed the island's protective coral rim racing towards her, she suddenly realised what he had been shouting. 'The reef. You won't make the reef.'

She hung onto the control column for dear life and somehow the plane listed clear with only barest suggestion of a scrape against the treacherous coral. Perhaps the high tide or the difference in their weight had been enough to give her a chance. For a moment her mind went blank with relief, then the realisation that the sea was rushing by not more than a few feet below her jerked her back into action and training took over and she began to fly the plane, climbing to the height she had been given and turning onto the heading for Mustique.

As she banked and headed north she saw Griff, still standing in the inlet, his hand shading his eyes as he followed her progress. A victory roll would have been a satisfying touch. Perhaps it was just as well she hadn't the faintest idea how to accomplish such a thing. Since she had met Hugo Griffin she had taken more than enough risks to last her for the rest of her life. And she still had to make her first ever landing on water.

It was perhaps more of a splash-down than a landing, but both Maddy and the aircraft survived the experience. Just. One of the floats had been damaged on take-off and as she taxied to the jetty she had the distinct sensation that they were getting heavier in the water. She climbed out and saw with a lurch of anguish that the little craft was listing. But there was nothing she could do. He would find it there. Or someone would tell him where it was. It no longer concerned her.

She was halfway down the jetty when she remembered the cheque. She retrieved the envelope and stuffed it into her bag and then walked up to the villa. Someone would drive her to the airport.

★　★　★

That afternoon, in Barbados, she spent the afternoon in her hotel defiantly indulging herself in all the things that she had been denied while on Paradise Island. Spoiling herself thoroughly. Taking a grim satisfaction in doing precisely what Griff would most despise her for.

But, despite having her hair and nails done, wallowing in the most expensive scented bath oils she could find and then spending a ridiculous amount of money on a dress to wear on the plane home, there was precious little satisfaction in the looks she attracted as she hesitated in the lobby of the hotel. She still had two hours to get through before leaving for the airport, but didn't want a drink, couldn't face food — she didn't think she would ever be hungry again. She wasn't anything. Just empty.

'Maddy?'

She swung around at the sound of her name, but it was too late to hide. 'Rupert,' she said unenthusiastically.

'What are you doing here? I thought you were with your aunt.'

'Godmother,' she corrected him, shaking her head. 'A change of plans. I'm going home tonight. In fact I really should go now and get my things together.' She made a move, but if she had hoped to be off-putting she had failed.

'On the BA flight?' Rupert asked, following her. 'I'm booked on that. Perhaps we could share a taxi out to the airport.'

'Rupert — ' she protested helplessly.

'Maddy, please,' he begged. 'I know I behaved like an idiot and I'm sure I'm the last person in the whole world you want to be with, but frankly, if you don't mind my saying so, you look ghastly.'

'Thank you, Rupert,' she said, but with a flash of humour at his total inability to say the right thing.

'No,' he muttered, embarrassed. 'Lovely dress, everything perfect. Just — something about the eyes. Has something happened? Your father's all right? That isn't why you're — ?'

'No,' she said quickly. 'It's nothing like that. Rupert, I know I apologised for the way I spoke to you, but — '

'Maddy, don't; you're making me feel worse than I already do . . . Oh, look, come and have a drink. You needn't tell me anything, but you don't look as if you should be on your own. And if you'll promise to forget what an idiot I made of myself I'll promise I won't embarrass you by proposing again.'

'Do I look *that* bad?' she asked, her sense of humour finally getting the better of her misery.

'You could never look that bad,

Maddy. I made a fool of myself, not that that matters — I'm always doing it — but I upset you and I'm sorry for that. Put it down to these hot tropical nights . . . '

'Positively dangerous,' she agreed, with feeling. 'I don't deserve you to be so kind.'

'You deserve — ' he began urgently, then stopped. 'Well, to be happier than you look.'

She gave a little sigh. Perhaps it would be better not to be alone. 'An orange juice, then.'

Rupert grinned like a pleased puppy and Maddy remembered why she had found him so charming the first time she had met him. He wasn't threatening or demanding, which was why his sudden change in character had taken her so utterly by surprise. And he was soon chattering happily about the test match he had just watched — nonsense to take her mind off her troubles. He was so kind that she was forced to make an effort to appear to be diverted.

'Would you like a drink, madam?' The stewardess said, beaming at her shortly after take-off.

Maddy forced herself to relax. It was ridiculous, she knew, but until the doors of the great jet had closed, shutting out the soft tropical night and the ripple of a steel band somewhere in the distance, she hadn't felt quite safe. Why on earth would Griff follow her, for heaven's sake? This morning he hadn't been able to wait to be rid of her. She found a smile for the stewardess. 'I'd like a mineral water, please.'

'Would you make that two, Susie?' Maddy felt her skin contract at the shock of his voice. She couldn't look, refused to look. It couldn't possibly be him.

'Sure thing, Mr Griffin. Nice to have you aboard,' Susie said and swung smoothly away.

'I'm afraid there seems to be some

confusion over seating arrangements,' Griff continued, producing his boarding card and addressing Rupert. 'You appear to be sitting in my seat.'

Maddy, her eyes fixed firmly on the seat ahead of her, put her hand on Rupert's arm. 'Please stay where you are. I'm absolutely certain that Mr Griffin will be perfectly happy in the seat he occupied during take-off.'

'I boarded at the last moment and had to sit in Economy. I did, however, request this seat especially.'

'Did you? This seat? Is it special?' And Rupert, groomed from the nursery in the conduct of a gentleman, stood up and reached for the card in his top pocket to consult the number.

'Very special. You see, I suffer acutely from a fear of flying . . . Unless I sit next to a qualified pilot I'm inclined to panic.'

'Good Lord,' Rupert said; then, as he sensed the tension that sparked between them, saw Maddy's stark pallor, he suddenly realised that something was going on between the two of them that was far above his head. But he latched onto something he did understand. 'But Maddy isn't a qualified pilot,' he said, clearly hoping that this would settle the matter once and for all.

'Oh, yes, Maddy is,' Griff replied, with the absolute conviction of a man who knew what he was talking about, and he swung into Rupert's place alongside Maddy, stretching out his long legs as he settled in beside her.

'I say — ' Rupert protested — at this cavalier hijacking of his seat, at the possessive manner in which Griff took Maddy's hand, apparently oblivious to the way she flinched away from him.

'The thing about Maddy,' he continued, his tone confidential as he directed his remarks to Rupert, 'is her remarkable shyness about her accomplishments, but friends at the West London Aero Club tell me that she has been the keenest student. She gained her licence after the minimum number of flying hours and was pronounced an exceptional student by her instructor.'

Griff had checked up on her? That easily? Maddy finally turned and stared at him and found herself drowning in the cool challenge of his eyes. Somehow she had expected him to look just as she had last seen him — bare-chested, wearing nothing but a pair of scruffy shorts and ancient leather flip-flops, a faint shadow on his chin where he hadn't shaved. But he was clean-shaven, wearing a well-cut, tropical-weight suit in cream linen, his shirt open-necked, but his tie was draped around his collar as if, in his rush to catch the plane, he hadn't had the time to knot it. It was silk, an extraordinary and very beautiful blend of the colours of the sea around Paradise Island.

And on the hand holding hers was a signet ring, plain gold, but in the clear light at thirty thousand feet she could see the tiny griffin engraved upon its surface. How could she have ever been so stupid not to have realised? He had walked Paradise Island like a god, not like some casual trespasser.

'Is that true, Maddy?' Rupert demanded from the aisle, jolting her from her reverie. 'Can you fly?' He was astonished but clearly very impressed.

Griff answered for her. 'Take my word for it. Everything is true, except the fact that she's an exceptional student.' His jaw tightened ominously. 'In my opinion she's reckless in the extreme, takes quite unnecessary risks, and any landing that needs a crane to rescue the plane from the sea . . . '

'I haven't yet learned your trick of doing it with the power turned off.'

'Come back to Paradise and I'll be happy to teach you.' He turned to Rupert. 'The thing about Maddy is that once she gets the hang of a thing she's such an enthusiastic student.'

'Maddy . . . ' Rupert muttered as they began to attract the attention of the other passengers. 'I don't understand. Do you know this man?'

Maddy was quite unable to answer. The numbness had finally gone and she was hurting. He was toying with her like a child twisting unwanted spaghetti around a fork and the pain was so intense that it was impossible to give words to, but she couldn't take her eyes off Griff.

'Well, Maddy,' Griff encouraged her, 'answer the gentleman's question. Would you say that you *knew* me?'

Her cheeks were scorched by a fierce blush. How could he be so hateful? What on earth was he doing here anyway, tormenting her? He'd had his fun; what more could he possibly want from her?

But Rupert was waiting, agog at the barely sheathed hostility between them. 'We met briefly when I was flying to Zoe's,' she said, carelessly, because it was essential that Griff should never know how much he had hurt her.

Griff extended his strong, square-cut hand to Rupert. 'Hugo Griffin.'

'But Griff will do,' Maddy said cuttingly, and then wished she hadn't as he turned to face her and raised a brow in a tiny acknowledgement that her barb had found its mark and would be repaid with interest. Before he could say something outrageous she said, 'May I introduce my companion? Rupert Hartnoll.' Something happened to Griff's eyes. The green became slaty and despite the fact that there was not the slightest change in his expression the tightening of his grasp upon her fingers betrayed how much effort it took to keep his feelings under close restraint. The knowledge went to her head like a rocket and she added, 'You'll recall that he asked me to marry him . . . '

Out of the corner of her eye Maddy saw Rupert stiffen and hated herself for using him. But he didn't let her down. 'As soon as you say the word, old thing . . . '

'Covering all your options, Maddy?' Griff asked softly, and her whole body gave a little jerk as she realised what he was implying. 'But then the full moon is notoriously fecund.' Did he truly believe her capable of foisting another man's child on poor, unsuspecting Rupert? And yet, if he thought that, he would surely never bother her again? He would leave her alone to try and put her life back together, relieved no doubt to be rid of any responsibility. For a long moment he regarded her, his eyes scouring her face, ransacking her mind to discover the truth. She kept her face quite blank, walled up her heart against him. 'Don't even consider it, Maddy. I'll not allow another man to bring up a child that I have fathered.'

He wouldn't allow? What the Dragon Man wanted, he took? 'What will you do, Griff?' she demanded. 'Breathe fire?'

He didn't answer, but removed the signet ring from his little finger and, taking her left hand firmly in his, slipped it onto her third finger and held it there. There was a terrifying finality about the gesture.

'Take it back,' she said, panic-stricken. 'I don't want it.' But when she tugged at the ring it wouldn't budge. 'It won't come off.'

'Anxiety makes the body swell,' he advised her. 'That's why small boys get their heads stuck in railings.'

'Then I'll summon the fire brigade and get it cut off,' she threw at him, a little wildly.

'No, you won't, Maddy. You're mine and you know it. There's no escape.'

Maddy felt herself being swept away on a rising tide of panic and she had to put a stop to it, do something before she did something really stupid like throw herself into his arms. 'If you don't go this minute and leave me alone, Griff, I'll scream,' she said very quietly. 'You were very impressed with my scream. It was convincing . . . you said.'

For a moment he continued to challenge her, then, clearly impressed with her determination to carry out her threat, he rose to his feet. 'You have a scream that could cause a riot. Not wise at thirty thousand feet. And I like flying with this airline.' He reached into the overhead locker for a blanket and draped it around her, tucking it in as if she were a child. Then he touched her cheek gently. 'You look tired, Maddy; try and get some sleep. I'll have a car waiting when we land. And once we're on the ground you can scream all you like, I promise.' He straightened, nodded briefly to Rupert and walked away, found a seat somewhere behind them where, thankfully, she couldn't see the way his hair curled into his neck, or the beautiful shape of his ear . . . A little sob escaped her lips.

'Maddy . . . ?' Rupert asked as he resumed his seat, his voice so gentle that she flinched.

'Don't!' she begged, and beneath the blanket she gave a little tug at the ring that was a shackle holding her fast to the Dragon Man. It stubbornly refused to budge. Her stupid trick finger wouldn't let it go.

The stewardess returned with their drinks. 'Ah, you have all sorted out the problem with the seats? That's good.'

She beamed, bearing Griff's mineral water away.

Maddy's glass rattled against her teeth as she swallowed her drink and she was grateful — deeply grateful — that Rupert chose not to say anything. Later she would try to explain. Later. But the tears were rolling down her cheeks and Rupert put his arm around her and drew her onto his shoulder. 'Maddy, love . . . ' And without meaning to she found herself weeping silently into his lapel.

'Oh, Rupert, I'm sorry, so sorry to have involved you in that.'

'Don't fret. I'm sure it'll all sort itself out . . . and if it doesn't, if you really wanted me to marry you I dare say I could force myself,' he said, passing her his handkerchief with an encouraging smile. 'No matter what Griffin says.'

'Oh, don't,' she wailed unhappily into the soft linen. 'I couldn't feel any worse.' But as the hours passed and they drew closer to their destination she felt a great deal worse. And when she went to freshen up the fact that Griff was stretched out in his seat in the relaxed posture of someone deeply asleep did nothing to set her mind at rest. It suggested total confidence that he had everything under control.

'He can't make you go with him,' Rupert insisted. 'I'll take you home. Or wherever you want to go. You could stay with my mother if you like.' She shook her head, but when Rupert stood up she asked nervously, 'Where are you going?'

He smiled a trifle absently. 'Don't worry, I'll be back in a moment.' And when he returned to his seat beside her a few minutes later he would not be drawn, but when the plane taxied to a standstill, the stewardess, all concern, ushered Maddy to the exit ahead of the other passengers.

'How did you manage that?' Maddy demanded.

'I told her you were on your way to a clinic for a life-saving operation.'

'And she believed you?'

'Next time you pass a mirror, Maddy,

look in it. You're so white under that tan that you look as if you're about to suffer from liver failure.'

'Oh.' Then, glancing nervously behind her, she added 'But it won't help; we'll have to wait for our luggage.'

But Griff, although hard on their heels as they approached Immigration, didn't appear in the luggage hall and, having reclaimed their bags, Rupert steered her firmly towards his waiting Rolls.

'But what could have happened to him?' Maddy demanded as they were whisked into London.

'Maybe his passport was out of date. Will you be all right?' he asked as he dropped her off at her flat.

'I'll be fine. I just need a little space and a good night's sleep.'

'Well, if you need me, you know where I am.' He paused, then said, with half a smile at his own foolishness, 'But you don't need me, do you, Maddy? You need him.'

10

Despite a restless night, Maddy decided to go into her office the day after her return. Anything had to be better than sitting at home dreading the ring of the bell in case it was Griff on her doorstep. Anything had to be better than sitting there longing for him to be there.

'Your holiday doesn't appear to have done you much good,' her father said, when he dropped by later that morning. 'Maybe you picked something up. Better see a doctor.'

'It's just jet lag. I didn't sleep very well last night. How did you know I was back?'

'Zoe telephoned to make sure you were home safely.' Maddy felt her whole body jolt. She would have to face Zoe, but right now she didn't feel strong enough. 'She said there was some kind of mix-up at the airport?'

'Mix-up?'

'Was someone supposed to give you a lift?' He didn't wait for her answer, impatient with such trivia. He propped himself on the corner of her desk. 'So, did you find out what's going on with Hugo Griffin?'

'Dad — '

'He can't be after her money. He owns an enormous transport company. Air, sea, car hire — you name it.'

'Yes, I discovered that for myself. Is it sound?'

'I wish I had a piece of it; the man has a genius for organisation apparently.' Then he realised that she was serious. 'Have you heard something?'

'No. But Zoe gave him a cheque.' She told him the amount and he whistled. 'The thing is, I . . . I've got it. I don't know what to do with it.'

'How on earth . . . ?' he began, then apparently thought better of it. 'Send it back to her. She's had time for second thoughts; it's more than most of us get . . . ' He stood up to leave. 'Oh, by the way, she wanted me to give you a message. Apparently your phone was off the hook.'

'I didn't want to be disturbed.' Her father gave her a rather hard look. 'What was the message?'

'She said to tell you that she's sorry about what happened, that she'll explain when she sees you and that you mustn't, on any account, marry Rupert Hartnoll. For any reason.' The unasked question hovered in the air.

Sorry? Maddy felt like laughing at the inadequacy of the word, but it wasn't Zoe's fault that Maddy had lost her head in the moonlight. 'Well, you can tell her not to worry. I'm not going to marry Rupert. I'm not going to marry anyone,' she added, with a determined set to her jaw, and she gave the dragon ring a surreptitious twist, to no avail.

'No?' Her father tried hard to hide his disappointment. 'Well, of course, that's what I told her,' he said. 'But she seemed absolutely convinced. I believe the woman's wits are wandering. She should get married again; it would give her something to occupy her mind.'

'That's terribly chauvinist of you, Dad!'

'Well, that's me,' he said. 'I can't pretend. What you see is what you get.'

'Don't ever change,' she said, standing up quickly, turning to stare out of the window so he shouldn't see the tears that suddenly stung her lids.

Her father joined her at the window. 'I wish you could find someone, Maddy — ' Then, as she took a deep, shuddering breath, he asked, 'What is it?' He looked more closely at her. 'Hey, girl, come and sit down. What ever is the matter?' He settled her on the sofa where she conducted informal interviews and poured her a glass of water, but she shook her head. 'Tell me, sweetheart,' he said, sitting beside her, taking her hands.

'It's difficult.'

'I've never known you to back away from a problem.'

'Oh, this isn't like me at all.' She

gathered herself, tried to hold in her mind that moment on the beach when she had recognised a moment of absolute truth, a moment she had promised herself she would never regret. Well, fate, it seemed, was determined to test her to new limits. She tried a smile and found that it wasn't as bad as she feared. 'The thing is . . . I wondered . . . since you want to be a grandfather so badly . . . would you mind if I managed it without actually getting married . . . ?'

Her father looked at her, rather hard. 'That, I take it, is not a hypothetical question?'

'It's too soon to be sure.' And yet she knew, had no doubt that she was already nurturing a tiny life within her. 'No,' she said, with sudden conviction. 'Not hypothetical.'

'Was that what Zoe meant? That you shouldn't marry Rupert just because — '

'It wasn't Rupert,' she said quickly.

'Are you going to tell me who — ?'

'It . . . it doesn't matter, not now. I

shan't even tell him.'

'I see.' Her father frowned.

'You don't think I'm right?'

'It's your decision, I suppose, but . . . well, if it was me, I would want to know.' He patted her arm. 'I'll be here for you, you know that . . . I just wish you had your mother to advise you . . .' He paused. 'I had hoped you would see more of her if you decided to go ahead with the Paris office. I suppose that's on hold?'

'I hadn't thought about that, but I suppose so.' Then she gave his shoulder a little shake. 'Once I tell her my news, she won't be able to keep away. Perhaps it's a good thing. This way, you'll get to see more of her too.'

'Do you think so?' He covered her hand with his own. 'Look, you should still be on holiday; why don't we both go to Paris this afternoon and break the news to her? Maybe, if we can show her how much we need her, we can persuade her to come home with us.'

★ ★ ★

Maddy dropped her bag, closed the door of her flat and leaned back against it. It had been wonderful to make her peace with her mother, wonderful to see the spark between her parents rekindled, but it was a relief to be home and be able to stop smiling, stop putting on a brave face for the world.

Her hand was full of mail, mostly Christmas cards she had picked up from her box, and she flicked through them, but there were no envelopes with handwriting she didn't immediately recognise. Relief and pain in equal amounts assaulted her. Had he come to the flat while she had been away? Gone away when he realised she wasn't there, flown back to Paradise? Well, wasn't that what she wanted, why she had so eagerly grasped the escape her father had offered? She tossed the mail onto the hall table. She would look at it later; right now she needed a shower and a cup of tea, in that order.

She was under the shower when she heard the house phone buzz and she decided to ignore it. But it rang again — an urgent little tattoo that demanded attention.

She wrapped herself in a towelling robe and pressed the button. 'Who is it?'

'Maddy? It's me, Zoe. Can I come up?'

Maddy held her breath for a fleeting second, wanting to refuse. But it was nearly Christmas. The season of good-will. 'Of course,' she said, and pressed the front door release, opened her own front door and then retired to wrap her dripping hair in a towel.

She heard the front door close. 'I'll be with you in a minute, Zoe,' she called. 'Can you put the kettle on? I've only just this minute got back from Paris.' There was no answer, but she heard the water being drawn in the kitchen. She walked back in. 'Mum came back with us . . . '

Griff was hunting through the kitchen cupboards and as her voice died away he turned to her. 'Where do you keep the tea?' he asked.

'Where is Zoe?' she demanded.

He produced a hand-held recorder from his pocket and pressed 'play'. 'Maddy? It's me, Zoe. Can I come up?'

'You — ' He raised a warning finger and she bit off the insult that sprang to her lips, standing back from the door to leave the way clear. 'Go away. Get out of here, or I'll call the police.'

'Come on, Maddy, you've already pulled that one,' he said, without rancour. 'I've proved myself a pillar of society ten times over so it won't work again.' He turned back to the cupboard, opening a series of storage tins. 'Oh, here it is. Why is it in a tin marked . . .' he looked at it with a puzzled expression ' . . . Tapioca'?'

'They both begin with T,' she said faintly.

'There's a somewhat baffling logic in that, I suppose. But why — ?'

'What did you mean, I've already pulled that one?'

'Well, not the police. Customs. It was really very clever; I was impressed with your ingenuity.' He concentrated on pouring the boiling water onto the tea. 'They held me for twenty-four hours before I managed to convince them that I wasn't an international smuggler — '

'What?'

He turned to her. 'It wasn't you?'

'I couldn't have done that,' she whispered, horrified.

'But apparently you know a man who can . . . ' He shook his head. 'Who would have thought Rupert Hartnoll had it in him?'

'Who indeed?'

'And when I had finally extricated myself you had bolted. To Paris, you said? With Hartnoll?'

'I went to Paris to see my mother. Why are you here, Griff?'

'You know why I'm here. To marry the mother of my child. The Christmas holidays will slow things down, but we shouldn't leave it too long. I have to get back — '

'Go back now, Griff. I don't need this. I don't need you.'

'And the baby? A child needs two parents — you know that.'

'I know what it's like to be deceived, deluded, lied to . . . '

'Don't be so hard on her, Maddy. Zoe thought she was doing something to help.'

'Zoe? I wasn't talking about Zoe. I was talking about you!' Then she sank onto a kitchen chair. 'Oh, Zoe, what have you done?'

'She called in a favour. I once made her a promise that if I could ever do anything . . . if she needed anything . . . I would be there for her . . . '

Promises to keep. For a moment she was back in the cool forest, surrounded by flowers, and the scent of the frangipani was almost real. 'So, what did she ask you?' she demanded, jerking herself back to the present.

'To teach you a lesson. Make you think about other people.'

'And, having witnessed my rejection

of poor Rupert, I can understand why you found it so easy to be unpleasant, rude, downright horrible to me. You thought I was a really nasty piece of work and you were going to teach me the lesson of my life.' But did you have to make me fall in love with you as well?

'Zoe was very convincing. You had been spoiled by money and now that your father had decided to put his fortune into a trust you had become a monster. She knew you, Maddy. I didn't. And, as you say, I had the evidence of my own eyes.'

'But she knew . . . '

'About Andrew? Yes, she admitted as much when I spoke to her. But Zoe had a hidden agenda. She was certain that if we were thrown together . . . that if there was no escape . . . She was right, Maddy. When I walked into the clearing that first morning and you were standing there under the shower I thought my heart would burst.'

'I would never have known.'

'You'll never know how hard it was to keep it up. I tried to tell you how I felt . . . when we climbed to the top of the island.'

How could she ever forget that moment, that kiss? 'And what about afterwards?' she demanded.

'I thought you had guessed. You said . . . I don't know . . . something about Zoe and I was convinced you had realised who I was. And, having discovered that I was not just some penniless charter pilot but the Dragon Man, you threw yourself at me. Anything I wanted, you said, and I knew then that Zoe was right. I hated you for that . . . and I hated her . . . I lost my head . . . '

'I had no idea who you were. I thought you wanted money from Zoe, that you were going to hurt her. I'd been there, Griff. I wanted to save her from that.'

His face creased in a puzzled frown. 'But why on earth did you think that?'

'When you came to Mustique with

306

Zoe, Dad and I . . . ' She swallowed. It seemed so ridiculous now, in retrospect. 'We assumed that you were Zoe's lover.'

'Lover!'

'Zoe was asking Dad about selling stocks and he was suspicious . . . You were so much younger than her . . . And then I found the cheque.'

'You have it?' She nodded reluctantly and fetched her bag. The crumpled envelope was still where she had thrust it and she handed it to him. 'I'm about to launch a scholarship fund for the island children. Zoe wanted to be a part of it.'

'I see,' she said very softly.

He glanced sharply at her. 'Do you?'

'So no one else's mother will have to work themselves to death . . . ' She couldn't go on. 'Well, that's it. You kept your promise, Griff. It's over now.'

'It will never be over, Maddy,' he said, and moved towards her.

'No,' she cried a little desperately as the warm scent of his body seemed to invade her spirit, weakening her resolve.

She pushed him away, retreated to the sitting room. 'I don't want to hear this. I just want you to go away and never come back.'

'Why?'

'Why? Can't you understand how betrayed I felt?' She could hardly breathe with the pain of it. 'I stood on the veranda of a house that you told me didn't exist, listening to you talking to Zoe on a radio that could have had us off the island an hour after we landed. Except that was no part of your plan. After all, there was no emergency. There was nothing wrong with the plane; it had all been a clever little plot to teach Maddy Osborne to be a good girl. Well, you taught me, Griff.' She raised her chin and lashed him with her eyes. 'Tell me, how good was I?'

'Maddy — '

'Not that good, apparently, because you couldn't wait to get me off the island.'

'For pity's sake, Maddy, if I was so anxious to get rid of you why do you think I followed you? Why have I been kicking my heels around a cold, damp city when I could be in the sun?'

'Guilt?' she demanded.

He raked long fingers through his hair. 'Sit down, Maddy. Listen to me.'

Maddy, beyond arguing, sat down, ready to repulse him if he came too close, but Griff sat on the chair opposite her, leaned forward, his elbows on his knees, and began to speak. 'Have you any idea of the fright you gave me when you took off from the island?'

'I wasn't thinking about your feelings at the time,' she said. 'In fact I can guarantee that what you were suffering was very much at the bottom of my list of priorities.'

The muscles in his jaws tightened. 'I suppose I deserve that. But I had no idea that you could fly — you never said a word — and my head was full of pictures of your body mangled in the wreckage. I couldn't blot them out. I had no idea where you'd go, if you even knew where you were going . . . I put out a call and when I had word you had arrived in Mustique . . . '

'I'm sorry about your plane, Griff. I know how much it meant to you.' He didn't answer. For a moment it seemed as if he couldn't speak, and Maddy held out her hand halfway, but his eyes were closed and with a little gasp she snatched it back. 'I was going to tell you that I could fly,' she said crisply. 'If you hadn't been quite so rude I would have asked you if I could have taken the controls for a while . . . But you were so forbidding, so angry.'

'That, my dear girl, was because I was already half in love with you and yet I had to believe Zoe, do what she asked — '

'Why? Just what is it between you two?'

'I met Zoe when I flew her down to her villa ten years ago. All I had was that little seaplane and a dream.' He looked down at his hands. 'A dream,' he repeated, very softly. 'She encouraged me, helped me with contacts, introduced me to the right people — the people who could smooth the path — and when everything might have failed at the last minute she stepped in to guarantee my loan with the bank. Without her there would be no Dragonair, no Dragon Man.'

'There is no Dragon Man,' she said, accusingly. 'This is a griffin.' She held out her hand. 'The head and wings of an eagle, the body of a lion. I've been living rather closely with it for the past few days.'

'When we were deciding on a name for the company Zoe suggested that a dragon sounded more exciting. Who has ever heard of a griffin?'

Maddy nodded. 'So you believed her.'

'Only with my head. My heart went its own way . . . Come back with me, Maddy. Come back with me to Paradise.' He knelt before her, his hands on her shoulders, forcing her to confront the pain in his eyes, the dark rings beneath them that were an echo of her own. It was unbearable. He could make those eyes tell lies as easily as his lips — First when he'd wanted her body, now when he wanted her child. No matter what Zoe had told him, he should never have agreed to do what she'd asked. It showed an arrogance, a blatant disregard for her rights as a human being.

'But you couldn't wait to ship me out once you'd . . . ' Made love to me. She couldn't even say it; it was too painful.

'Zoe was going to come and fetch you on Sunday. That was the arrangement, but I couldn't carry on with the deception. Won't you try and understand?'

She shook her head. 'No, Griff. I will never understand. Not in a thousand years.' She stood up, walked away so that he shouldn't see her face. 'I think you'd better leave now,' she said stiffly.

'I won't let you go.'

'You can't force me to marry you simply because I'm expecting your child, Griff.'

'Then it is true?' His voice shook a little, but it took a moment for Maddy to realise what that meant . . . He had seemed so certain . . .

'It's far too soon to tell,' she said a little huskily. 'Please . . . please go, now.'

'But if you are really expecting my child — '

'It doesn't make any difference, Griff. You can't make me love you,' she said, a little desperately.

'You already love me. That's why you're finding it so hard to forgive me.' She could feel the warmth of his body at her back, but he didn't touch her. 'I could show you that now, Maddy. I could make you beg me to stay, we both know that,' he said as a convulsive tremor shivered her body. 'But I won't. We are one, you and I, for the rest of time. The moon was our witness.' He turned her gently, took both her hands in his and raised them to his lips. 'I love you, Maddy, and when you can find it in your heart to forgive me I'll be waiting for you. No time limit.'

★ ★ ★

'Maddy? It's Zoe. Can I come up?' Maddy hesitated before pushing the release. It had been a week since Griff had used a recording of Zoe's voice to gain entrance to her flat. A week in which she had heard nothing from him. He had disappeared, as he'd promised, leaving her to make up her own mind, but she wasn't taking any risks.

'Prove it,' she demanded suspiciously.

'If you don't let me in this minute, Maddy Rufus, I'll call everyone I know and let them know that your nickname has nothing to do with your hair but an incident with a tin of red paint . . . '

Maddy slumped against the wall. Lord, how she had wanted it to be him. Then, as the phone buzzed again, she realised that she still had not released the door. She pressed the button and a few moments later her godmother burst into the flat with a hug that said everything.

'What are you doing here, Zoe? If Griff sent you — '

Zoe held her finger to her lips in

mock horror. 'Darling, if he knew I was here he would never speak to me again. He made me swear I wouldn't try and influence you.'

'So?'

'I've come to grovel for your forgiveness on my own behalf. I know that it's entirely my fault that you're pregnant — '

'Don't be ridiculous, Zoe. I have a mind of my own. Besides, I'm not even sure that I am pregnant. It's far too soon to be sure.'

'There's no need to be kind,' she replied, with a shiver. 'Is there any chance of a brandy? In your shoes I would be sulking too.'

'I'm not sulking!' Then, more gently, Maddy said, 'You don't understand — '

'How could I? I wasn't there. But I'm sure it was perfectly dreadful. It was *meant* to be dreadful. Washing under that freezing shower, camping on the beach . . . I wanted him to feel *sorry* for you, want to comfort you . . . ' But Maddy hardly heard her. Mention of the pool sent her heart flying back there, to the touch of Griff's hands as he had washed her hair under the shower, the dizzy plunge at dawn when they had swum there after making love.

'Oh, Zoe, why did you do it?'

'I knew he was ready to fall in love with you. I saw the way he was looking at you the night we called on you in Mustique. The man's a born romantic. But you would have run away . . . '

A romantic? He had threaded flowers through her hair and kissed her and made love to her beneath the moon. And he had felt sick when his imagination had tormented him with pictures of her mangled body in the wreck of the plane. And he loved her. He was waiting for her. No time limit.

'Good heavens, is that the time?' Zoe said, leaping up. The sky had grown dark and as Maddy moved to close the curtains she saw the slender curve of a sickle moon behind the stark outline of the plane trees in the square. 'I must be going, Maddy,' Zoe said, touching her shoulder. 'I'm going to the theatre this evening.'

'Yes, of course. It's lovely to see you.'

'Well, I wanted a little chat. I hope I've cleared your mind a little.'

'It's a long way to come for a chat,' Maddy said.

But Zoe was searching in her bag. 'I almost forgot this.' She produced a package from her bag. 'I bought you a little present. Nothing much. Happy Christmas, darling.' She kissed her god-daughter and held her for a moment, then she was gone.

For a moment Maddy held the beautifully gift-wrapped parcel. She carried it across to the sofa, sitting down before she pulled the ribbons and opened it. It was a small furry dragon, bright red with a brave tail and tiny eager wings. She lifted it up and then touched it against her cheek and when, a long time later, she held it away she couldn't understand why it was wet.

★ ★ ★

The launch skimmed across the bright, sparkling sea. Maddy had set out at dawn from St Vincent and now Paradise was coming towards her out of the horizon. Approaching from sea level, it seemed larger, the small, central peak higher than she remembered. But it was, if possible, even more beautiful than she remembered.

As the launch neared the jetty she could just make out the house, adjust to the scale of it, appreciate the ingenuity that had gone into the design and construction. There were no hard edges to jar against the forest; the only bright colours were supplied by the flowers that tumbled over the roof and the veranda rails and softened the gentle slope of the path that led down to the white curve of the beach.

And Griff was standing at the end of the jetty, feet planted wide, arms akimbo as the launch drifted into the little bay. Maddy's heart caught in her throat at the sight of him, but he turned away to catch the rope thrown to him by the boatman, not meeting her eyes. He made the launch fast but as she moved to step up onto the jetty he blocked her way.

'Why have you come, Maddy?' he demanded.

Maddy had not known quite what reception to expect. Maybe not quite to be swept into his arms . . . but this? Shaken, she withdrew slightly from the eager movement that had carried her towards him. Because you were right. Because I love you. The words stuck fast in her throat. 'It's Christmas. I came to bring a present for Jack,' she said.

'Jack?' At least she had managed to surprise him, buckle that unwavering self-assurance.

She turned to the cage standing on the floor of the cabin out of the sun. Griff jumped down into the boat to examine the small brown parrot hunched unhappily on her perch.

'I've called her Jill. Not very original.'

He grasped the cage in one hand and her elbow in the other. 'Come on. Let's introduce them.'

A few minutes later Griff set the cage very quietly on the veranda below Jack's favourite perch up in the roof. 'I think we'd better leave them to it for a while.' He glanced at her. 'It's hot; can I get you a drink?'

It was all so very stiff and formal. Despite his urgent declaration in her flat, it seemed that he had changed his mind.

'A glass of water?' she suggested. They retreated to the kitchen, where Griff opened an enormous refrigerator powered by the solar panels on the roof.

'It's odd being in the sun on Christmas Eve,' she said, propping herself onto a high stool, attempting to achieve some normality in their conversation.

He was leaning against the units, arms folded, and as she nervously sipped at her water Maddy was aware that Griff's penetrating eyes never left her. 'Why did you come back?' he asked again.

'I told you — '

'Don't fudge it, Maddy. Don't use borrowed wings . . . ' He saw her confusion. 'You could have sent Jill by air freight with a Christmas card.'

She slipped down from the stool. 'I think I'd better go.'

'Won't you admit it, even now?'

'You're not making it easy . . . '

'I want you to be sure in your own mind that you want to stay here, with me, for the rest of your life. Despite everything I said, I don't want you to stay just because you're pregnant. I'll support you and I'll want to see my child. But I don't want you to have any illusions. Once I send the boat away there'll be no more choices to make. You'll be mine.' The lines that bit into his cheeks deepened. 'You must want to stay for no other reason than that. Anything else is impossible.'

'Do you want me to stay?' she asked.

He refused to give an inch. 'You know what I want, Maddy. I told you in London.'

A crash from the veranda, a flurry of wings took them through the door. The cage was lying on its side, the door open and Jill was sitting preening herself on top of it while Jack watched contentedly from the rail of the veranda. If only it was that easy for people, Maddy thought. No stupid pride, no need to hide your feelings in case you were hurt. She turned to Griff and he was looking down at her, waiting. It was that easy. Griff had bared his heart to her, had given her all the time in the world to make her decision and still she had lacked the courage . . . But she must find it from somewhere. It was too important.

'I love you, Griff,' she said. 'I came back because I wanted to be with you. I'm not even sure that I'm going to have your child . . . It's a little early to be sure . . . '

He seemed to be a little closer. 'If that's the only thing that's worrying you, my love, we could make absolutely certain . . . '

'Tell the boatman to go, Griff,' she said softly.

'What boatman?' She turned to the jetty, but the launch was already disappearing into the distance.

'You . . . ' She turned back to him. 'You've already sent him away . . . '

'You didn't think I'd take the risk of losing you again? Welcome to Paradise, my love,' he said with a soft laugh, and she smiled as, very softly, he enfolded her in his arms, kissing her until she thought she must surely cry with happiness.

We do hope that you have enjoyed reading this large print book.

Did you know that all of our titles are available for purchase?

We publish a wide range of high quality large print books including:
Romances, Mysteries, Classics
General Fiction
Non Fiction and Westerns

Special interest titles available in large print are:
The Little Oxford Dictionary
Music Book, Song Book
Hymn Book, Service Book

Also available from us courtesy of Oxford University Press:
Young Readers' Dictionary
(large print edition)
Young Readers' Thesaurus
(large print edition)

For further information or a free brochure, please contact us at:
Ulverscroft Large Print Books Ltd.,
The Green, Bradgate Road, Anstey,
Leicester, LE7 7FU, England.
Tel: (00 44) 0116 236 4325
Fax: (00 44) 0116 234 0205

THE HOUSE ON THE SHORE

Toni Anders

Roderick Landry, a war artist suffering the after-effects of the trenches, stays for a few weeks at the Cornish hotel where Elvina Simmons lives with her aunts Susie and Tilly. Initially reserved, Roderick eventually warms to Elvina and to life in the sleepy little seaside village. And when, together, they renovate the ruined house on the shore, it seems that their friendship may deepen — to love.

JUST IN TIME FOR CHRISTMAS

Moyra Tarling

Vienna was just a girl when she came to live with Tobias Sheridan and his son, Drew. But when a bitter family feud sent Drew packing, he'd left town, unaware of Vienna's secret passion for him . . . Now he was back. A widower, Drew had returned for the holidays with the grandson his father had never known. But when he took the lovely, grown-up Vienna in his arms, he knew he'd come home at last — just in time for Christmas.

THE SECRET OF HELENA'S BAY

Sally Quilford

Shelley Freeman travels to an idyllic Greek isle to recover from a broken romance. When elderly Stefan von Mueller disappears soon after speaking to her, she's drawn into a disturbing mystery. Everyone else at the resort, including handsome owner Paris Georgiadis, claims never to have seen Stefan. Shelley starts questioning her sanity, and then fearing for her life, as wartime secrets start to unfold. She soon wonders if she can trust Paris with her heart — and with her life . . .

VERA'S VALOUR

Anne Holman

Vera's life, as a wartime bride and British Restaurant cook, is thrown into turmoil when she is handed a vitally important message for her Royal Engineer husband — just after he has departed for D-Day preparations. She eventually catches up with him, but danger is all around them and she must find her own way home again, leaving Geoff to his duties — and without having given him an important message of her own . . .